Who Pissed Off Ivy Dell?

Indie Sparks

Twice Shy Publishing

Before You Begin:

If you've not yet read books 1 and 2, you want to detour here and go do that first.

This part of the story will welcome you back when you are ready.

~

"The desert could not be claimed or owned- it was a piece of cloth carried by winds, never held down by stones, and given a hundred shifting names."
- *Michael Ondaatje*

Ivy
The Work of a Wizard

I'm no expert on signs or omens, but I feel like finding a dead bird on your doorstep probably doesn't mean anything good. It's such a small bird, too. Is it a sparrow? Oh, please don't let it be a sparrow. Shit, this feels personal. Intentional. Who have I crossed? And who in Ivydell would sacrifice a sparrow just to prove a point?

Don't be an idiot. An animal did this. Probably that badger you scared off your back patio. Vengeful fucker.

I nudge it with the toe of my shoe to be sure it's dead. Oh, yeah, this frail little birdie has flown for the last time. There's a wound in its side, but its filthy feathers prove it didn't go down without a struggle.

Wait a minute. Those feathers don't look real. It's a . . . it's a toy? Like, a cat toy? It's lifelike from a distance, but I don't think it was ever alive. I toe it again to flip it over. Definitely a cat toy. Real birds don't have tiny bells inside them. Not usually. But where would a cat have come from?

Myrna steps out of her casita and waves from across the street. "Morning, doll! Whatcha studying over there?"

"I thought it was a dead bird, but I think it's just a cat toy."

"Ah, Wizard left you a present."

"A wizard?"

"April's cat. Have you met April yet?"

"No."

"Well, then it makes sense that you haven't met Wizard either. You had coffee this morning?"

I shake my head and start walking toward her place, stepping over the gift from Wizard. Making coffee is normally high on my morning priorities, but I thought I heard thunder when I came out of the bathroom, so instead of going to the kitchen, I stepped outside to look at the sky, and then I got sidetracked by the dead cat toy, and now my whole day is off to a weird start.

At home, I'd never leave my house looking like I'd just stumbled out of bed. But this is Ivydell, and I do a lot of things differently here. I'm different here.

Me and my bedhead cross the dirt road to Myrna's. She hugs me like she always does, her head barely coming to my shoulder. Unlike me, she doesn't have a hair out of place. Her sleek, platinum hair swings over her shoulders as she goes up and down the stepstool she uses to reach the cups in her cabinet. Physically, she needs a boost, but her personality takes up space. Her voice, too.

"Who would let their cat wander around outside here?" I ask. "A hawk could carry it off."

"That hawk would have to be on steroids," she says, bringing our full cups to her small table. "Wizard is a Maine Coon. Purebred. Big guy."

I look up from my dry cuticles that I've been inspecting as she sets our coffee on the table. Then she positions her arms as if she's ready to cradle a toddler in them. That can't possibly be an estimation of Wizard's size.

"No domestic cat is that big, Myrna."

"I'm telling you, he's big. And talkative."

"He can talk?"

"Don't be a smartass. You know what I meant. Cat talk. Chirps and yowls and purrs. Noisy, but he's sweet." She takes a sip of her coffee.

"Hmm, Jensen says his owner can be difficult. Care to elaborate?"

"Oh, April's a pain in the ass."

"Did she know Gran?"

"No, she wasn't around back then. She's only been in Ivydell for five years. Patrice would've put her in her place right quick, though."

"What does she do that bothers everyone so much?"

"She's one of those people who likes to be heard, even when she doesn't really have anything to say. Never knows when to shut up."

"Like her cat."

"You'll see. Speaking of talk, how's Stinger's dirty talk game?"

I groan, but I do it with a smile. Myrna is always trying to get me to reveal intimate details about Jensen. I don't think she really wants to know. She just wants to make me blush. And laugh. I'm really going to miss her when I'm gone.

"You know y'all are never going to get rid of me, right? I'm always going to come back."

"Oh, yeah? As what?"

"No, not come back due to reincarnation. I mean here. In this life. I'll come back to Ivydell. Even if Jensen and I decide not to try the long-distance thing. I'll still come back to visit."

My stomach burns after the words leave my mouth because I

really want us to try for the long-distance relationship, but I know we can't make a final decision until the time comes. Of course, we want it now, but there are realistic things to consider. It wouldn't be easy, but I can't imagine not trying. I don't think my attraction to him is just because we met here. I think I would've fallen for him on the beach or in a bar or at the grocery store—anywhere.

I can't think of a single place where I wouldn't have been drawn to him. We'd still be us in the real world. It's not just the magic of Ivydell.

Myrna's concerned expression makes it clear she's worried about me, probably thinks I'm going to get my fragile heart broken. Maybe I will, but I'd rather know we tried, even if prolonging the heartbreak makes it ten times worse when it ultimately happens. I have a pattern of sabotaging things whenever I start to feel attached, but it's different with him. No part of me wants to wreck this.

"I'm going to be okay," I say. "Even if it ends."

"Everything ends, doll. That's how new things begin."

"To new things." I lift my cup to her.

"To bold new horizons," she says, which is such a Myrna thing to say.

When we finish our coffee, I ask if she needs anything from the store. She says no, says she went yesterday and stocked up because she's going to do a little stress baking today. But she won't give me a straight answer when I ask why she's stressed.

Must be the festival. There's a growing buzz in the air. Mostly, it feels exciting, but I've felt some unease in the wind lately, too.

Myrna walks me to her door, and I shriek when I step outside. "Look!"

"Yeah, I guess it's about time for those adorable little shitheads to start coming around again."

"My first chipmunk sighting."

"I think those might actually be ground squirrels," Myrna says. "But people around here insist on calling them chipmunks. I don't guess the cute little rats care either way."

"If Jensen calls it a chipmunk, it probably is one. He's a stickler for animals being identified correctly."

"Is that right?"

"Whatever you do, don't call a bison a buffalo in his presence."

"I'll make a note of that."

"But if he says it's really a squirrel, I'm still going to call it a chipmunk because I like it."

"And because it will agitate him, and you like that, too."

"Why would I like agitating him?"

"I can't imagine." Her lashes flutter as she rolls her eyes.

I snap a picture of the chipmunks before I head back to my place, and text it to Jensen.

> Is this technically a chipmunk or a ground squirrel?

> You're going to call it a chipmunk no matter what I say.

> Aw, it's like you know me or something. What are you doing?

> *About to head over to the community center for the meeting.*

> *There's a meeting?*

> *Not for you. Just for the regular residents.*

> *Oh, okay. I need to go to the store, anyway.*

> *Drive safe.*

> *I will.*

I know what he meant about the meeting not being for me, but it still sucks to be reminded I'm technically an outsider. I pay rent. I've helped clean and plant, and I've repainted all the signs for the casitas. But I'm temporary, and everyone else is a *regular* resident. How many years will I have to come back temporarily before I'm seen as a regular part of this place? Will it ever happen?

Jensen

Mirror, Mirror

I linger in the community center for a while after the meeting adjourns. I've got a list of things people want me to fix, but I need a moment to breathe in the familiarity of this space before I get started. This was always supposed to be temporary for me.

My thumb taps the image Ivy sent earlier. She's going to miss those little rats when she goes home. Maybe I'll miss them someday, too, but I bet it would take a long time.

Dice comes back inside. "Hey, if the Spirit Sisters had something they needed you to take care of, put them ahead of me on your list."

He has a soft spot for the old women. He's known them a long time, and he's basically a nice guy in general.

"Okay. Thanks. Theirs is minor. Your septic issue might take a while."

"You know I'll help. I'll go rattle Cujo's cage if we need another set of hands."

"I'll probably try to recruit him on my way to your place. Might not mention it's septic work." We both laugh. "Hey, you never told me if you had to face her at your last tournament."

Dice runs his hand through his hair. "You know, it's a hell of a thing to look across the table at the only woman who could ever outplay you. Full-circle, right back to the way we met. I knew before we even got started that she held the upper hand."

I know he means that in every way possible. Then and now. "Eh, you'll win the next hand."

He shakes his head. "I might be done. When one thing changes, why not two?"

"Careful. They say bad things come in threes."

"Yeah, but they say that about good things, too. See you in a bit."

As much as I'd like to avoid them today, I park in front of Whispering Winds, home to the spooky sisters, Alma and Elma, and their spirited business.

Elma opens the door. "Hello, there. It's kind of you to come so quickly."

"Yes," Alma says from somewhere behind her. "Ours wasn't an urgent request, but we are eager to have the mirror hung. Though its usefulness here may be limited."

I am not about to encourage her to explain what she meant by that. It could have simply been a reference to how much longer they'll be able to interact with ghosts here, but it also could've meant they believe there is something otherworldly about the mirror itself, and I don't need to know anything about a haunted mirror. Especially not if they plan on freeing something from it.

The mirror in question is an antique. A very heavy one. Screws alone won't hold this. I'm going to have to anchor it. I hate drilling into these old adobe walls. Patching holes in them and getting a good match on the color and texture is impossible. Not that it really matters at this point.

If the sisters want this mirror hung, I'm going to hang it for them.

When the job's done, the twins come up behind me in the mirror to admire it. The three of us are reflected in it, me with my hair sticking out from under my Giants ballcap, and them with their long, gray braids . . . we look like we're from completely different eras.

But we've been a part of the same community for the past four years, all three of us falling more and more out of touch with the way people live outside our fences.

It's always been odd. But I owe a hell of a lot to this place and these people.

"Is there something special about this mirror?" No idea why I couldn't just leave well enough alone, but I can't take the question back.

"Yes," Alma says. "I felt a special connection to it the moment I saw it."

I knew it.

"All mirrors are special," Elma says. "Because our mirror images are how we see ourselves. Photographs are how others see us. Those can be edited to tell whatever story we want people to believe, but the person in the mirror is the one we must learn to love unedited."

Alma nods. "And images in photos preserve a moment in time. But the you in the mirror is constantly changing, always evolving."

The thought of standing around, watching myself age makes working on Dice's septic system look better by the second. "Well, if the mirror is all you needed, I'll move on to the next person on my list, and let you ladies get on with your day."

"Before you go," Elma says. "Look into the mirror again."

She steps aside, out of the reflection, and then Alma steps away, too.

"Do you see him?" Elma asks.

"Who?"

"The man you've become," Alma says. "She sees him. She's proud of him. But she doesn't want him to stop becoming the man he's meant to be."

"And she says you aren't meant to be alone."

I suddenly smell Jenna as distinctly as if she were standing right next to me. I don't see her in the mirror, but her scent . . . ten seconds ago, I couldn't have described it, but memories are powerful enough to fuck with your senses. To make you believe it's not your imagination when a small detail comes rushing back and hits like a goddamn helmet to your knees.

"I don't guess it's healthy for anybody to be alone too long," I say, nodding at the sisters as I walk toward the door, not meaning to dismiss them, but not wanting to hear more of their spooky life lessons either. It's too much. My hand turns the doorknob, but I realize I can still smell her, so I hold still.

I hold on.

She's here, but there's an unseen force pushing at my back, a voice telling me I have to go, that the past isn't a home. It's a photograph. A moment in time captured in an image. Millions of beautiful moments preserved in millions of beautiful images. All forever unchanged.

I've spent the past four years trying to remain unchanged, knowing all along that life isn't meant to be like that. It makes no sense to know something with absolute certainty, but still doubt it with everything you've got. Denial is easier sometimes, but the truth doesn't change.

People change. It's how we're meant to be. Moving, but with purpose—not trying to outrun pain, but learning to grow past it without looking away from it. To leave it behind without running from it. So many things I've known, yet refused to accept.

But not needing to run? That's more than a shift in perspective. That changes how I breathe. It shoves the boulder off my back, not because I choose to accept it, but because it makes the choice for me. It leaves me like a fever breaking—cold sweat, weak limbs . . . sudden clarity.

I wasn't just running to escape. It was the only way I ever knew to be. I've never felt like I wasn't in a race—whether it was to stay at the front of the pack so my dad would see me or to escape the reach of his sight when I wanted him to stop focusing on me or to keep the cruelest pain from gaining on me.

Until this beautiful moment right now.

I'm standing still. All of me. And I'm okay.

Even here in Ivydell, hidden away from responsibilities and obligations, I've been running. But right now, I don't feel like I have to do anything bigger or better or faster or harder, or hide or fight. There's no fear or anger thrumming in my veins. No strategizing for survival.

No need to run.

I step back to the mirror for another look. Because I need to see it in my own eyes to trust it.

The change is undeniable. I see it for myself.

Petra

Scaling Back

THE TONE OF THE knock alerts me it's April. The moment I shut her down in the meeting, I knew she'd be showing up at my casita to finish making her point. I fling the door open, ready to shut her down again.

"Oh, Ivy. Hi. I thought you were going to be someone else."

"Nope. No such luck."

It's not just her knock that's snappy tonight.

"I didn't mean to imply I wasn't happy to see you. What's on your mind?"

"Just wondering if there was anything I could do to help out tomorrow."

"What's tomorrow?"

"It doesn't have to be tomorrow, specifically, Petra. Just if you need anyone to do anything soon to help get ready for the festival, I'm available."

"Well, thank you, but you've done a lot already. And I appreciate it. We all do. But you've got a job to keep up with, too. I don't want your time here to have a negative impact on your real life."

"I can manage my work schedule and still contribute."

I try to choose my words carefully. She's too much like Patty to accept a placating response. She's got that sixth sense. "To be honest with you, we're scaling back a little this year. There will be more to do, but nothing right now."

"Why are you doing less this year?"

"You put on an event long enough, you ultimately learn some things." I laugh at myself, and it's genuine. "We never really needed to go all out with the decorations. It's a lot to clean up and store after the festival is over. Some of us are getting too old for all that."

"But you've got Josephine, Cujo, and Jensen. And me, even though I'm not a *regular* resident."

"Is this about the meeting?"

"No. I mean, it does kind of sting to not be included, but I understand that not everything in Ivydell concerns me. I just want you to know that I still want to be a part of things. As much as I can be."

"You truly have no idea how much I love that you are here for this year's festival, Ivy. I promise I will let you know every time there is any prep to be done."

"Thanks. But let's don't scale back, okay? I think Gran would've wanted me to experience the festival at its most over-the-top level possible."

Oh, she's good. Knows just when to play that card. And she's right. It's exactly what Patty would want. It's how she'd want us all to experience it.

"Maybe we won't cut back as much as I'd planned. We have fewer artists this year, though, so we don't want to overhype it. I want it to be clear when people arrive that it's smaller. Don't want anybody thinking we pulled a bait and switch on them."

"Why are there fewer this year?"

Well, at least I know Jensen wasn't texting her the minutes of the meeting when he kept looking at his phone.

"Like I said, hon, people are getting older."

"If you put the word out online, you could get artists to rent space for the festival. Probably more than you have room for."

"It's a little late for that."

"Maybe next year. I could build a website for the festival and create an application for interested artists. You could rent out any available casitas to them, and I bet Jensen could renovate some used campers for temporary housing."

"Whoa, there. You don't let any grass grow, do you?"

"Sorry. I get excited, and I love planning things. I used to help Gran with an arts festival at home. She was on the planning committee, and then she became the head of the planning committee, and then she took on so much of the work that it became a one-woman committee."

"She never got over that, huh? When we were together, she was always volunteering for shit, and then taking up everybody's slack until she was the only one doing any damn work. God, it used to make me so mad when she let people run roughshod over her like that."

"Yeah, but she wasn't good at delegating because she couldn't let go. She felt responsible, so she maybe micromanaged a little."

"They say we recognize our own traits in others." I smile at her because there's no way she doesn't already know she's just like Patty in that way.

"Well, they say we're attracted to our own traits sometimes, too."

"Are you saying you think Patty and I had that in common?"

"I honestly don't know how two control freaks ever had a relationship. Except you at least make sure people do the work they signed up for instead of doing it for them."

"And that right there was the key. We were a lot alike, but we were just different enough."

"To drive each other crazy?"

"Far too often. But every now and then, our strengths meshed. Those were good times."

"I'm sure your strengths would've worked together more often as you got older if . . ." She looks stunned at what she's said or what she was about to say. "I'm sorry. I didn't mean that to sound like—."

"Don't apologize, Ivy. I know exactly what you meant. And I like to think you're right."

And I wish I could include you in meetings, but my old heart won't let me.

"Let me know when there's something else to be done for this year's festival, but next year, I'm on the planning committee. And I won't take no for an answer, so don't even think about shutting me out."

"I promise that won't happen."

Ivy

Little Nudges Everywhere

I LOOK UP FROM my phone and see the big cat coming toward me. It's not a mountain lion. It has long silvery hair. It's a Wizard.

Not wanting to spook the floofy kitty, I look around, pretend to be uninterested until we're close enough to each other that I can almost reach out and touch him. I squat down and extend my hand. "Hey, Wizard. It's nice to meet you."

He closes the distance between us and rubs his head against my hand.

"Oh, you're a sweetie, just like Myrna said." His meow is loud with a hint of a screech to it. "She was right about you being noisy, too."

The enormous cat purrs as I drag my fingers down his back. "Oh, listen to that growly purr. Are you a lion? Is that what you are, Wizard? A big, silver lion?"

"How do you know my cat?"

The voice startles me. Damn, she's stealthy. Wizard's back arches as if she's surprised him, too.

I stand to introduce myself. "You must be April. Hi, I'm Ivy."

"Oh, so you're Petra's little darling, huh?"

"Excuse me?"

"I heard about you already, that's all. You're the granddaughter."

"What else have you heard?"

"Well, let's see. I'm supposed to be nice to you. Not comment on your affair with Stinger—"

"Affair? Neither one of us is married, so we're not having an affair."

"You're scrappier than I expected." She pulls her head back and examines me from head to toe. "Taller, too."

"Who described me as meek and short?"

April laughs and runs her hand through her hair. It's the color of a paper grocery bag, darker than beige, but not quite brown. She's shorter than me, but average height. Most everything about her seems fairly nondescript. Except her personality. Her attitude probably surprises a lot of people when they first meet her. Thankfully, I've been warned.

"Nobody called you meek, just sweet."

"I can honestly say no one described you that way."

She laughs harder at this. "Well, good. Then I won't disappoint."

Josephine's car slows so we can step out of the road and let her pass. She waves at me through the windshield, but she doesn't stop, doesn't even roll down her window.

"Figures you'd be friends with her."

"What does that mean?"

"Aren't you friends?"

"Sure, I'd say we're friends."

"Well, there you go. It was nice to meet you, Ivy. Come on, Wizard."

The cat follows her. Very doglike. I think I'll buy him a toy to replace the destroyed one he left on my doorstep.

I knock on Josephine's door. April may not have wanted to explain their beef, but I need to know.

"So, I see you've met April."

"I met Wizard first. And then she appeared out of nowhere, asking how I knew her cat."

"Owning that cat is her most redeeming quality."

"What's the deal between y'all?"

"She thinks she had something going with Cujo and I messed it up for her."

"What does Cujo say?"

"He says everybody makes mistakes, and she was one of his."

"Ouch. I hope nobody calls me a mistake."

"They wouldn't. He's nice to her, just not nice in the way she wants him to be, and that pisses her off, so she blames me."

"Were they a couple or just—"

"More like a couple of times."

"Oh. What's weird is that she doesn't seem like the clingy type. More like she'd push everybody away."

"Yeah, well, she wants to cling to Cujo."

"He definitely doesn't seem like he'd be into a stage five clinger."

"Not at all."

"That's why he's into you. Your independence."

"How do you know it's not my excellent blowjob skills?"

"I'm sure that doesn't hurt. But the free tattoos are probably the real draw."

"I haven't tattooed him."

"Why not?"

"He's never asked."

"Wait a minute. You showed up at my door with your kit, saying you desperately needed to tattoo someone like it was an addiction. You've never asked him?"

"He has an artist. A talented one. I don't know." She shrugs and looks away. "He might not think I'm good enough."

"You won a competition on a TV show. You're business partners with a famous tattoo artist, and if that guy thinks you're good enough, why wouldn't Cujo?"

"He doesn't really pay attention to other people's standards. He has his own."

"But he's never said he doesn't think you're good enough, right?"

"And I don't want to give him the chance."

"You're good enough, Josephine. For anybody and anything. You're good enough."

"Thanks. But coming from someone who won't let me tattoo her . . ."

"I don't let anyone tattoo me!"

"I'd probably never question my worth again if you'd trust me to be the first."

"Nice try."

"Dammit."

"April might need some ink."

"Sure. I'd definitely be her first choice."

Josephine needs to know Cujo thinks she's good enough. I think his opinion might hold more weight than anyone else's. I wonder if he realizes that.

It's not like I'm going to tell him. Not outright, anyway. But maybe he's good at picking up clues. If someone were to just drop a few hints, he'd probably catch on in no time. He probably just needs a little nudge.

Jensen

Dinner Talk

THE SEPTIC WORK AT Dice's would've been so much worse without Cujo's help. If we're lucky, it was the last time any of us will have to patch a field line. His system is old, but the repair will keep it functioning for a while longer.

Ivy's been quiet today. I check my phone again. Still no new texts, not even a link to a video she's sure I'll find as funny as she does. She's usually right. Her silence either means she's catching up on work or hatching a plan. The last time she went a whole day with no contact, she was repainting signs. She might've been a little pissed off at me, too.

I can't think of anything she'd be mad at me about today, though. And there's no sign left untouched.

You got plans for dinner?

What did you have in mind?

Popcorn?

Come on over.

Oh, you expect me to deliver it?

I tip very well.

Can't argue with that point. I search my fridge and freezer for something that could actually count as dinner. We're definitely starting with popcorn, but I'm going to want something more substantial afterwards. All I've got is eggs. And cheese. Omelets? Not that I can make a fucking omelet. I can scramble them, though. Cheesy scrambled eggs it is.

I add a bottle of wine to the bag and head out.

Ivy opens her door with a smile, her hair is still damp from the shower, and there's a sun-kissed glow on her cheeks. She must've spent some time outside today. I want to touch her warm skin, breathe in the smell of her shampoo, and taste her kiss, but I also want to memorize every detail about her standing in the doorway, smiling at me like this.

"That's a big bag for popcorn."

"I brought dinner, too."

"Oh, yeah? What are we having?"

"Cheesy scrambled eggs and wine."

"Classy."

"Damn. I should've left off the wine." I step forward and claim her mouth with mine. The kiss is aggressive, and she matches my intensity. "I was kind of in the mood for trashy this evening."

"Would you settle for a classy slut?"

"Is that like an average slut, but with a nice glass of wine in her hand?"

"Who are you calling average?"

"Not you, beautiful. You are a superior slut." I kiss her on the forehead and step past her.

She follows me into the kitchen. "Did you bring butter for my popcorn?"

"Of course. You're not dealing with an amateur here."

I open the wine and pour us both a glass. She trails her tongue around the rim to tease me while we wait for the kernels to explode. "You keep doing things like that and you're going to end up with burned popcorn."

Her laugh is seductive, and I don't even think she's trying. "No meteor shower tonight," she says. "What am I supposed to look at while I eat my popcorn?"

"You'll see stars. I promise."

The first kernel pops, and she jumps a little, which makes her giggle at herself, and that makes me laugh. "Somebody's jumpy tonight."

"Maybe she's just really excited about the appetizer portion of the meal." She puts the butter in the microwave.

"I know I'm looking forward to it."

She hands me a bowl, and I dump the popcorn into it. Her hand looks so delicate as she pours the melted butter over it. Mine are rough, and they bear more than a few scars, but hers are smooth, unmarred except for one small white V on the side, near the base of her thumb.

"How'd you get that scar?"

"Broke a glass while washing dishes. I forget it's even there."

Bringing her hand up for closer inspection, I kiss the thin scar. It's so symmetrical, it almost looks intentional. "Even your scars are beautiful."

"So are yours."

I know she meant something deeper, but I hold her hand next to mine for comparison, anyway. She pulls our hands toward the popcorn bowl. "You have to stir the butter."

Her hand plunges into the bowl. I shake in some salt, and then my hand follows hers. We toss the popcorn around, our fingers colliding, lifting a mountain of popcorn until some topples over the edge.

We take turns feeding each other, and I'm having a harder time than usual taking my eyes off her tonight. But I'm ready for hers to close, so I make her see stars.

She brings her wine, but leaves the popcorn in the kitchen, when I pull her toward the bed. I laugh to myself at the amethyst figure she keeps on her nightstand, facing away from her pillow because she's been a little unsettled by it ever since the spooky sisters gave it to her. And more so since I turned it around to face her in the middle of the night. I'm going to turn it around while she sleeps every chance I get because it's funny, but there really is something slightly unnerving about it.

I take Ivy's glass and set it next to the not-angel-maybe-ghost amethyst woman.

"Lie down."

"I can't. You haven't undressed me yet."

"Such a brat, making me do all the work."

She bites her lip and shrugs. "Hey, you want access, work for it."

"Work for it, huh?" Dropping to my knees, I yank her shorts down her long legs, discovering she didn't bother with panties after her shower. Her bare pussy is perfection. I tease my tongue into her seam and trace her clit until it starts to swell. Her fingers sink into my hair, but I stop and stand again.

I pull her t-shirt up, already knowing she's not wearing a bra. The anticipation of seeing her tits has my mouth watering, but I pause before the reveal. She's watching my face, but I can't peel my gaze off her body to make eye contact.

Her nipples are erect, and they harden further when the air hits her skin as I remove her shirt. My thumbs tease over them, and I groan as they firm up even more. I take one into my mouth, and she moans, lacing her fingers into my hair again. I squeeze her ass, and she rises onto the balls of her feet, her back arching, pushing her breast harder against my mouth.

I slide over to suck her other nipple, and her fingers clench in my hair. Her ass cheeks contract in my hands as it happens, making me wonder if her pussy is clenching, too. I release her ass, and then immediately slap the left cheek. "You ready to lie down yet?"

She sits on the bed and begins to scoot backward. Once her calves are on the mattress, I grab her ankle to halt her, pull her leg up and slide two fingers into her pussy. "So fucking wet. And tight."

I stare down at her while I continue to finger her. "Do you like this?"

"Yes, Daddy."

"Really? You're going to be a good girl for me so early?" I force a third finger in, knowing she's not entirely ready for it.

She gasps, winces at the fullness, but she continues to tease. "Is it too soon, Daddy?"

"Never." I ream her harder. "Is this too much?"

"No. But it's not what I want."

"Tell me."

"I want your mouth. I want you to lick my pussy until I see stars."

"I can't get into position until you do." I remove my fingers, lower her leg to the bed, and let go of her ankle.

She slides back and shifts her body, readjusting until her head is on her pillow. I sit on the bed and take off my shoes and socks, and pull my shirt over my head. When I stand and drop my pants, she spreads her legs so I can take my place between them.

While I was fucking her with my fingers, her juices spread over her lips, and they're still glistening as my face comes nearer. I lick over them and her hips rock. She stills when my tongue probes her opening. Her sweet arousal coats my tongue, and I can't get enough of the taste of her as I lick and tease out more of her essence. I stay there for a while, devouring her. Her soft moans tell me she's enjoying it, but this won't cast stars on the insides of her eyelids. There's only one way to do that.

I trace her clit with the tip of my tongue, flick over it a few times until her hips gently buck. My lips knead her clit, and then I caress it with my tongue as her hips circle. Then I draw her stiffening clit between my lips again and suck on it.

My name leaves her mouth behind a sound that is equal parts moan and whimper. Her hands fist the blanket, and her head lolls to the side. A few seconds later, her breath hitches and her ass quivers. My hands press against her inner thighs to keep them from closing in on me while her orgasm crests. She cries out and I suck harder, showing her all the stars.

I glide my tongue back down to her opening and taste her sweet cum. My mouth skates through her delicious slick release, avoiding her sensitive clit to allow her a chance to recover.

When her breathing falls back into a normal rhythm, I slide two fingers inside her and bring my tongue back to her clit. She lies back and lets me pleasure her a second time.

"Do you want another one?"

"I want you to fuck me, Jensen."

"How do you want it?"

"However you want."

I rim her asshole with my fingers still drenched from her cunt. "Here?"

"There's lube in the drawer. Condoms, too."

"Roll onto your side."

She rolls over and bends her top leg, dragging her knee up to increase my access.

I open a condom, roll it down my hard dick, and rub lube over it. Then I squirt some onto her and work it in with one finger. She tenses a little, so I go slow, adding more lube. When her muscles relax for me, I push my finger deeper. After a minute, I work a second finger into her the same way.

"It's been a while since I've done this," she says.

"You okay?"

"Yeah. I want it, just want you to know I might need a little more time to adjust."

"I won't rush." I start to slide my fingers in and out. "Is this all right?"

"Yeah, that's good."

She thrusts back onto my fingers, and I stop moving them so she can set the pace. It feels so damn good to have her rocking her ass back to take my fingers. When she picks up the pace, I hold out for a few more minutes before asking, "Are you ready for my dick?

"I think so."

I remove my fingers slowly and position the head of my cock against her tight ass, pressing the crown inside until she tenses again. Holding steading, I kiss her neck, and whisper, "I'm going to stay right here. Push back when you're ready. You're in control now."

Her body softens, and after a few minutes, she slides back, taking me a little deeper. And then a little more. When I'm all the way in, I close my eyes and get lost in the bliss. She slowly slides off, and my breathing shallows. She thrusts back to take it again, still moving slowly, but she doesn't stop to adjust to the fullness at any point. I'm reseated with one smooth thrust.

"You're doing so good. It's all you, baby. Take what you want."

Her strokes speed up a little, and she doesn't pause at the bottom, anymore. She's found an easy rhythm and it's fucking amazing, but it takes all my restraint not to meet her thrusts yet.

When she starts to moan, I push my hips forward. "Is it okay if I join in?"

"Yes, Daddy. Please."

Oh, sweet Jesus, is she trying to kill me? I manage a few strokes, but the more her muscles loosen, the quicker mine tighten. I knew I wasn't going to last long, but I didn't expect to blow this fast. "I can't hold it, Ivy."

"Don't hold back. Come in my ass, Jensen."

Every muscle and tendon in my body seize when she says my name with my cock buried in her ass. It's not like I have the power to resist doing exactly what she told me to, but it might be the greatest goddamn release I've ever felt. I'm pretty sure my soul just left my body.

After I regain enough strength to take my cock out of her, she rolls onto her back and smiles at me. "I'm going to grab a quick shower. You can join me if you want. And then you can cook us dinner."

"You might have to help with dinner. I'm not sure I could crack an egg right now."

She twists her hair up in a clip and steps under the hot water. I step in after her. A woman has never been safer from sexual advances in a shower with me. Until she soaps up her tits and my dick reactivates like it just got a new battery.

"Uh-uh," she says, glancing warily at my emerging erection. "I need a break. And food."

"You're the one who woke him up."

"Hot water's all yours." She hops out and grabs a towel.

My dick is the only muscle that's come back onboard. The rest of me is still drained. I laugh at how quickly she retreated though. Good to know she thinks so highly of my stamina.

By the time I dry off and come out of the bathroom, she's stolen my shirt. I reach for my underwear but don't both with anything else. I take my wine glass from the counter where I left it. She's eating the popcorn by the fistful and her glass is half-empty.

"I cracked the eggs," she says, pointing to the bowl they're floating in. "So don't say I didn't help."

"Go sit down so I can scramble them. You're distracting me again."

She pulls one of the chairs out from her table and turns it to face the kitchen. Then she sits cross-legged on it, making my shirt rise up to her hips, revealing just enough of her snatch to make my dick twitch.

"You're mean."

"Are you sure that's the word you were looking for?"

I take a drink of my wine and stare at that entire chair full of sassy gorgeousness. And then I turn around and get started on our gourmet dinner. "I meant beautiful. And mean."

She comes back into the kitchen and drops two slices of bread into her toaster.

"Guess what? I'm going to be on the planning committee for next year's festival."

My body locks from head to toe again, but it's a far less pleasurable sensation. "How'd you decide that?"

"Petra and I decided together."

"Oh. Okay."

I'm certain with every cell of my being that she has misunderstood something, but I'm not going to tell her that. I can't tell her that. There's no way to say it that wouldn't sound demeaning.

"And I'm about to play matchmaker for Cujo and Josephine."

"I think you might be showing up a little late for that job."

"Not matchmaker between a man and a woman. Matchmaker between a man and a tattoo artist."

"She was a tattoo artist when they met. What am I missing here?"

"She wants to give him a tattoo, but she doesn't want to bring it up because she's afraid he might think she's not good enough."

"You might want to let them work that out on their own."

"I think he just needs a little nudge in the right direction."

"You're going to nudge Cujo?"

"Gently."

"Oh, well, as long as you're just butting into his business gently."

"I'm not butting in. I'm helping. There's a difference. I met April today."

"Damn. You had an eventful day."

"I did. Is it true she and Cujo had a thing for a while?"

"Is that another issue you plan to help with?"

"No. But she shouldn't hate Josephine because of it. I feel like they could be friends if everybody just cleared the air, you know?"

"That's definitely a matchmaker challenge you should leave alone."

"We'll see. I need to get to know her a little better to be sure, but my instincts are usually good."

"Let's eat. Drink some wine. Get some sleep. You might have a whole new perspective by morning."

"Maybe. My ass will probably still be sore, though."

"You look so refined and sweet, and then you say things like that."

"And you like me even more."

I laugh into my wine glass. She's not wrong.

Ivy

The Art of Attraction

I'VE SENT MOM AT least a dozen videos of chipmunks playing, even though I know she saw them growing up. She hasn't told me to knock it off yet, so I assume she's enjoying them as much as I do. And she didn't correct me and say they're ground squirrels, so obviously, they've always been chipmunks here.

I wander into the community center to see if Tawny left behind any muffins from this morning. Sometime, she leaves a covered plate on the counter after they close up the coffee shop. I'm surprised to find her still there. She and Leo have set up easels near the front windows.

"Sorry. I didn't mean to barge in."

"Nonsense," Leo says. "We don't own this space."

"We'd paint outside if we could, but the wind makes it's impossible some days. We just want to get a few more pieces done before the festival, but you're not bothering us."

I spy the covered plate on the counter. "I'm glad I didn't disturb your process, but I'll be out of your hair as soon as I steal a muffin."

"You can't steal what's free," Leo says.

"Please, take the rest," Tawny says.

There are three left on the plate. "Maybe I'll take the last two over to Alma and Elma."

"You are so sweet," Tawny says. "I bet they'd love an afternoon snack."

Pausing at the door, I watch the couple paint for a few moments. I always loved watching Gran at work. When I was little, I'd sit and watch her for hours, stunned when her strokes turned into a recognizable image. Even when I was a teenager and no longer amazed by her process, I still loved coming home to find her on the sunporch with a paintbrush in her hand, humming in front of a canvas. She was so happy when she was painting.

I can't resist stepping over to see what Leo and Tawny are creating. His painting is abstract, and I like the colors, but I don't know much about this type of art. All I can say it's pretty.

Tawny's piece is a desert landscape with a cactus in bloom. The flower is bright yellow, but thin enough that there's sunlight coming through it, and she's set a haze of dirt in the wind so realistic I instinctively squint when I first look at it. The sky is the perfect shade of blue. She's not painting a sunrise or sunset, no magical melding of jewel tones.

This is the desert in midday, captured in its ordinary, dusty beauty. Tiny red flowers on a spindly stem, a white butterfly, brown and gray rocks. There's a pair of chipmunks I almost miss, so lifelike they look like they may run across the canvas any second. Every detail is so perfect it almost looks like a photograph. She's really good. And I really want this painting.

Gran mostly did watercolors. Her art is beautiful, but it presents the world the way you might want to see it, soft and full of illusion. Tawny's work is all stark reality. No illusions, almost commanding of attention. *Look at this. See these things. Appreciate them.*

"Are you going to sell this piece?"

"With any luck."

"Someone will buy it. Do you mind if I ask the price?"

She sets her brush down, but she doesn't turn to look at me. "I never set a price until a piece is done."

"Oh. Well, I'd love a chance to consider this one when you're ready to put a price on it. I don't know that I could afford it, but I really love it, and the sooner I know the cost, the sooner I can start figuring out a way to buy it because I'm pretty sure I'm going to think it's worth whatever you're asking."

"I wouldn't want you to put yourself in a bind over it. That wouldn't feel right to me, sweetie."

"You forget that an artist helped raise me. I wouldn't see this painting as an expenditure. I'd see it as an investment, and not just financially. It makes me feel. I don't care what anyone says, sometimes, happiness can be bought."

Leo clears his throat. "Amen."

Tawny just nods.

I leave them to get back to their work. A part of me wishes I'd never seen that painting because it feels like it's already mine, but I have no idea what Tawny's work sells for.

It may be nap time for the Spirit Sisters, and I don't want to disturb their rest. If Josephine's around, I bet she'll be happy to have one of these muffins.

Cujo's bike is parked in front of her casita. Yeah, I'm not knocking on her door when he's there. She doesn't knock on mine if she knows Jensen is over. I wouldn't mind as he's leaving, though, just long enough to casually bring up tattoos. Inconspicuously, of course.

Zara is going to love the coffee shop Tawny and Leo provide.

There is so much about this place that is clearly her vibe. I see it more and more since she said she wanted to come visit.

Shit. I never cleared that with anyone. Maybe Petra wants a muffin this afternoon.

I keep walking past my casita and Josephine's, around the corner to Petra's. She's going to get tired of seeing me on her doorstep.

As soon as I walk up, I hear the door bang on her hothouse around back. She sees me coming and shakes her head. I hold up the muffins covered in clear plastic wrap. "I come bearing baked goods."

"I don't take bribes."

"Well, hopefully, I don't need to bribe you. But I do need to confess something."

"Do I need to sit down for this?"

"How upset would you be if I invited a friend to come visit me?"

"Are you asking for permission or forgiveness?"

"Ummmm . . ."

"Is this a male friend? Am I going to need to keep Stinger extra busy while your friend is here?"

"No. It's a woman. And we are just friends. Zara really wants to see Ivydell. I didn't mean to overstep."

"This is the thing that makes you worry? Inviting a friend to come visit? You don't think twice about taking it upon yourself to repaint signs or about making plans for a website nobody asked for, but this has you worried."

"This involves someone else's feelings. I wouldn't want Zara to get the impression she wasn't welcome. She'd feel terrible, and so would I."

Petra smiles. "It's fine, Ivy. Your friend is welcome to come visit.

How long is she staying?"

"Four days. She took a week off, but she insists on driving, so she'll need two days for travel."

"She's welcome to stay in any of the unoccupied casitas you think she might like. Just let me know and we'll get it ready for her. To be clear, by we, I mean you."

"I assumed she'd just stay with me."

"You and Stinger can go four days without each other?"

"I hadn't thought about him in any of this. But Zara won't care if I see Jensen while she's here."

"Think about that before you decide. Plus, she might like to have her own space. To get the whole experience."

"That's true. The next thing we know, she'll probably be moving out here full-time, and I'll be the only one going back home."

Petra's bright expression darkens. I don't think she likes talking about me leaving.

"What kind of muffins are those?"

"They have cranberries, blueberries, pecans, sunflower seeds—"

"Just give me one. I'll waste away over here waiting for you to read me the ingredients list."

I unwrap the muffins and hand her one. "When I offered to help with the festival, I didn't just mean with the overall prep work. If you need any help getting your stuff ready, you know where to find me."

"You know how to distill tinctures?"

"No. But I can pour liquid through a funnel to fill bottles. Put labels on them. That kind of thing. And if you have the time and patience, I can probably learn how to do more."

"If you've got the inclination to learn, you let me know. In the meantime, I'll keep you in mind for bottling duties. Ask your friend if she'd like to stay in her own casita. I won't charge her anything. Don't go telling anybody else I said that."

"Got it. Thanks."

"Walk through my casita on your way out. There are some soaps on the table. Take one. Let me know what you think."

"I didn't know you made soap, too."

"I've got to use up all these herbs somehow."

"You should make candles. I know how to do that."

"I don't have supplies for making candles."

"You can get wicks and beeswax online. It can be softened with coconut oil so it'll burn more evenly and hold scent longer. And you don't need fancy jars; You can use small mason jars or silicone ice molds if you don't want to put them in jars at all."

"It doesn't take you long to turn a thought into a project, does it?"

"You said you had excess herbs to use up. I just like to help."

"I know."

"How are you packaging your soaps?"

"I was just planning on putting them all in a basket and letting people pick what they liked."

"Petra! You're not serious, right? Packaging has a huge impact on people's buying decisions. It can be simple, but it needs to be something. You could wrap them in wax paper. Secure it with twine and add some dried herbs for decoration with a cute little handwritten tag to label the scents."

"That sounds like a project you'd be great at."

"Oh, you don't even know how irresistible they would be when I got done with them."

"Fine. You are my official soap packaging designer."

"Don't forget about the candles."

"I never committed to candles."

"Candles hardly require any commitment at all."

"Okay, Patrice, Junior."

"Ha! My mom calls me that, sometimes."

"You don't say?" She takes a bite of her muffin.

I check out her soaps before I go. They smell incredible. I'm already thinking up names for them. She was probably going to label them with their literal scents, but these need creative names like Mystical Mint, Lavender Lullaby, and Me Thyme . . . I've got this. It's a good thing I came over when I did.

Jensen

Necessary Maintenance

April's list is the only one I haven't tackled yet, but I can't put her off any longer. Thankfully, there's not much to be done. I have a feeling some of what she's asking for is unnecessary at this point, but it might be easier to do it than argue with her. I'll do anything that's not absolutely ridiculous, but knowing April, some of her list will be.

I knock, and she calls out from the other side of the door to say she'll be a minute. A horned toad sunning itself on a rock lifts its head as if it doubts her estimated timeframe, too. I smile, thinking of Ivy's laundry encounter. She probably needs to do her laundry again by now. I wonder if she's gone to the laundromat to avoid using my machines.

> *I'll clear the lizards for you again if you need to do laundry.*

> *If you want me to come over, you could just ask.*

I wish. I'm at April's to tackle her repair requests.

Don't mention Josephine. She doesn't like her.

Yeah, someone should've warned you about that. Sorry.

I snap a pic of the horned toad on the rock and send it to her.

They're so much scarier in person.

Kind of like April.

The door opens, and she catches me smiling at my phone.

"If you're looking at porn, please shut that down before you come inside."

"It's not porn. It's a text."

"From your new girlfriend?"

She says girlfriend like it's a perversion of its own. "What do you have against Ivy?"

"Nothing. She seems okay, I guess. Terrible taste in friends, but she likes Wizard. He likes her, too, so she can't be all bad."

I spot the huge cat sleeping on April's bed, and for some reason, that makes me smile all over again. I'm sure Ivy does love that overgrown fluffball.

"There's no need to repair the fireplace crack," I say. "You can still use it. I marked that off your list, but I brought you a new showerhead."

"I want the fireplace repaired. It looks ugly, and I still live here, Stinger."

"You really want me to patch that for no reason?"

"I shouldn't have to look at a big, ugly crack every day, whether I'm lighting a fire or not."

"It's unnecessary, and I'm not doing it. Show me the broken floor tile."

She points out a tile in the kitchen where the floor meets the wall.

"No. I'm not chipping that tile out and replacing it because of a hairline crack. It's not a trip hazard. Even if it were a huge crack, it's by the wall. You're not going to walk over that. It's fine."

"As long as I'm paying rent, this place should still be maintained."

"I'm going to install your new showerhead. Is anything else malfunctioning? I'll fix mechanical issues, just not cosmetic shit."

"I'm going to complain to Petra if you don't at least fix the crack in the fireplace."

"Knock yourself out. I'll be in the bathroom if you think of anything else."

The new showerhead is bigger than her old one. She should be happy about that. It works great. I test the faucet on the sink to be sure it's not leaking. Works like a champ. Toilet flushes fine. No cracks in the mirror.

As soon as I come out of her bathroom, she tells me the seal on her patio door is worn out. The last damn thing I want to do today is replace the seal on a sliding door, but I check it. Technically, it probably does need a new seal. I caulk it.

"Is that a temporary fix?" she asks.

"Everything's temporary, April. Even us."

"You've been spending too much time around Cujo."

"Didn't come here to talk about Cujo." It's definitely time for me to leave.

"Is their relationship serious?"

"None of my business."

"He confides in you, though."

"I don't know why you think that."

"She just doesn't seem like his type."

"Right. Independent. Tattoo artist. Does her own thing."

"I'm an independent artist who does her own thing, too. Why not me, Stinger?"

Aw, shit. I knew better than to engage in this conversation. "There aren't rules about who people are attracted to. Anyway, I don't know that she wants anything serious any more than he does. That's probably part of the attraction for both of them."

"I half expected him to be gone already. He's always talking about moving on."

"He will soon."

"I know. It just sucks to think maybe he stuck around longer than he'd planned because of her. It's been a year. That's a long time for something casual."

"We've probably all stuck around longer than we intended."

"You got big plans for the future?"

"Nothing solid. Your shower is good to go."

"Thanks. I'm still going to complain to Petra."

"I'd be shocked if you didn't, April."

Wizard rolls over and meows. I wonder how much Ivy will like him when she finds out he's a chipmunk killer. She roots for the underdog. Undersquirrel, whatever. April definitely won't like Ivy if she finds out about the gentle nudges she has planned for Cujo.

she's just nudging him about a tattoo all she wants. I know exactly what's going on in her pretty head. And all too often, I think she knows what's going on in mine, too.

Ivy

No Drumroll, Please

I LOG OFF AND close my laptop. Even with the days I slack off, I'm still meeting my deadlines. But I dread them more and more. It's not that I don't want to work. I need a job; I'm just not sure how much I want the one I've got anymore.

I knew I was bored with it before I ever left for Ivydell. Bored and restless. Why else would I have packed up and hit the road so easily? But I didn't know how bored. I thought it was the same complacency everybody feels after a while on any job. Maybe it was. Still is?

Ivydell probably isn't the place to make big decisions about my life outside of here. But it wasn't just my job that I was bored with. I was hardly dating at all. Barely had any social life outside work, and when I went out with coworkers, I'd end up mostly hanging out with Zara and ignoring everyone else.

My apartment wasn't really a place I wanted to be either. Aside from the beach, I didn't enjoy being anywhere. I went where I had to go or was expected to go. Necessary places.

Ivydell doesn't expect anything from me. I'm unnecessary here, but I don't want to leave. Maybe I'm not someone who needs to be needed after all. Or maybe I was, but I'm not anymore.

I don't feel restless when I'm alone here. I still like having something to do, but I'm not bored. Doing nothing here doesn't make me anxious. I've learned to just be sometimes without wanting to crawl out of my skin.

And then there's Jensen. When we're together, I know it's because he wants to be with me, and I want to be with him, too. I'm never planning an exit strategy when we're together. It wasn't an instant attraction—okay, physically, it was—but I am so attracted to all of him now. His sense of humor, his grumpy moments, his generosity, his pain . . . I get it all.

The rest of the world would say we don't really know each other, but I do know him. Because he's let me, and he makes an effort to know me.

Opening up to someone new is usually a struggle for me, but it's easier with him. Will my walls go back up after I leave? Part of me thinks he's broken through them, but part of me is afraid I'll build them back stronger. I've done it before.

I need some fresh air. The breeze is warm and gentle this afternoon, and it smells clean outside. Not like soap or detergent, more plantlike, but not flowers. Almost herbal, but not quite that either. Green, but not as sharp as fresh-cut grass. Just fresh.

April is painting in her yard. She stands in front of a canvas on an easel, and I'd love to go over and see it, but she's prickly. Not sure she'd want anyone watching her work or peeking at an unfinished piece. I wave when she looks up. She returns the gesture, but she doesn't call me over.

There are prairie dogs skittering around on the edge of Cujo's driveway. A few of them are young. Gah, they're so cute. They start chirping when they see me approach. I'd love to think they're glad to see me, but they're warning the others. Tall redhead encroaching. Beware!

Cujo's screen door slams, and I suddenly want one of those. I'm going to ask Jensen if there are any in his shop. I'd love to be able to open my door in the evenings without having to worry about an animal wandering in.

"Why are you over here getting these rats all riled up?" he asks. His voice is as gruff as usual, but I know he's not mad. I actually don't ever want to see him mad.

"They're trying to warn you about me."

"I think they're at the wrong casita."

"It's too late to warn him about me."

Cujo laughs, and it's so loud the prairie dogs all freeze. He walks toward his bike.

"Hey, before you take off, can I ask you something?" I pick up my pace to catch him before he cranks up his bike and can't hear me.

His head turns toward me, but he's not smiling. "Why do I feel like I'm about to be ambushed?"

"No ambush, I promise. I was just wondering if you've ever thought about asking Josephine to give you a tattoo."

"That's a hell of a random thing to walk around wondering about."

"Okay, listen. If you don't think she's good enough, you can tell me, and I'll drop it. I'll never tell her that she's right about why you haven't asked. But if that's not it, maybe you could bring it up to her sometime."

"Does she want to give me a tattoo?"

"I can't speak for her. But as her friend, I don't think she'd say no if you asked."

"Don't do this shit. I need direct communication. Does she want me to ask her to do that?"

I nod.

"Are you refusing to speak now because you promised her you wouldn't tell me this?"

I nod again. "But maybe don't bring it up right away."

"How long should I wait?"

"Just whenever it feels natural."

"When do you suppose that should be?"

"In a few days, maybe? But don't make it abrupt. You know, just nuance it into the conversation."

"Oh, yeah. I'm all about nuance. Known for it." He straddles his bike and walks it back. I jump aside when it rumbles to life. He nods at me when he turns the handlebars, and then he smiles. I know that look. He's not smiling to be friendly; he's happy, and it doesn't have a damn thing to do with me.

Easiest nudge ever. Can't wait to tell Jensen how badly he underestimated me.

When I reach the rock-lined path that I helped clear, I step onto it to walk out to the circle. I don't know why, but I want to take a look and see if anything might need to be done out here.

The breeze blows through my hair, and a hawk circles in the clear blue sky. Such a perfect afternoon. More prairie dogs play to my left, making a sound I've never heard. Some of them are jumping and chirping as they run, but I hear a weird little drumroll sound, too. Like it's coming from farther back in their throat. Or maybe they do it with their tongues. It's not as loud as their other noises, but I know I heard some sort of vibration mixed in.

They've stopped making any sounds at all. I glance over my

shoulder to see that they've all vanished. They must have a burrow close by, but that was a quick disappearing act.

I see a few furry heads pop up. Their warning chirps sounds off again. And then the drumroll again, more isolated. I stop walking. It's not coming from behind me, which is where all the prairie dogs have gone. It's not a throat vibration.

That's a rattle. Fuck.

My eyes scan the dirt and scrub ahead. It camouflages so well, but I see the movement. It's not slithering toward me, but it's coiled and its head is moving. I hear Cujo's bike coming back. He must've forgotten something.

Please see me. Notice me standing still out here.

His bike goes silent. I'm afraid to take my eyes off the snake, but I have to know if Cujo sees me. He does. I can see him in my peripheral vision now, standing next to his bike.

"Rattlesnake?" he yells.

"Yes!"

"You're doing the right thing. How far?"

"Maybe six feet."

"Okay. You should be good. Hang tight."

"Yep. Not going anywhere anytime soon."

"Stay still. Keep an eye on it. I'm not going anywhere either."

I stifle a yelp when the snake lowers its head and uncoils. It's moving, I think. I hold my breath until I'm sure it's headed away from me. And then I start to walk backward in long, steady strides. There's probably enough distance between us now that I could turn around and run, but I'm afraid to attempt it. I take another step back. My foot comes down on a rock and something grabs me around the waist. I scream before I realize what's happened.

"You're okay. I've got you." It's Cujo. I stepped on his boot. He grabbed me to keep me from tripping. He was coming to my rescue, even though I'm pretty sure I'm out of harm's way. "You shouldn't be walking around out here in shorts."

"Thanks for the heads up."

He laughs, not as loud as usual. "They can strike through pants, but it's some protection at least. Bare legs are not a good idea."

"I've worn shorts before, and nobody said anything."

"It's not as likely you'd encounter a rattler up front where most of the casitas are. They're a lot more common out here in the open. They don't want to be near us anymore than we want to be near them. You did good, though. Somebody taught you enough to know you needed to hold still."

"We have rattlesnakes on the beach. They live in the dunes. There aren't a lot of sightings, but they're there. People see them more at night. I've always known what to do, but never actually had to do it."

"If I let go of you now, you can stand, right?"

"Yeah. Yeah, I'm good. Thanks." I hadn't even realized he was still holding on to me. I'm a little rattled for sure. "I think that puts an end to my afternoon walk."

"Come on. I've got to swing back by my place, and then I'll drop you at yours on the way out. You ever ridden on a motorcycle before?"

"Um, I grew up at the beach. Yes, I've ridden on plenty of motorcycles."

"All right. Good to know."

He mounts his bike and cuts his eyes at me. "Don't make my bike the first one you burn your leg on, please."

"I know how to get on." When my arms wrap around him, he drives off slowly. April is standing near the path, watching us. She must've heard us yelling back and forth about the snake. I wave.

She doesn't wave back. For a second, I'm afraid she's standing still because of a snake, too, but she turns and walks back in the direction of her casita.

Cujo goes inside to get whatever he'd forgotten, and then he drops me off at Sparrow's Song.

Jensen's truck is at Myrna's, so I walk across the street to tell them about my snake encounter.

Before I make it to her front door, she opens it, and she and Jensen stand and stare at me. "Listen, doll. You can't have 'em all."

"Cujo rescued me from a rattlesnake."

Jensen lunges at me from the doorway. "Are you okay?"

"Yeah. It didn't bite me. I knew to hold still, but it was pretty damn scary. Cujo saw me, and he watched until the snake moved on and I could back away. Then he came out to check on me and gave me a ride home."

"What were you doing hiking in shorts?" Myrna asks.

"Nobody told me not to. Until today. You're the second person who's mentioned it today."

"Let me be the third," Jensen says.

"Are people not allowed to wear shorts when they come to the festival?"

"We don't tell them what to wear, but we do tell them to stick to the path, and to pay attention to the signs."

"Signs?" I ask. "What signs?"

Jensen shakes his head. "We have warning signs, and signs to direct them."

"Where are they? Do they need to be touched up?"

Myrna laughs. "Uh-oh. Our official sign painter is warming up her brushes."

"You can take that up with Petra. Right now, I'm taking you home."

"Don't do anything I wouldn't do," Myrna says as she closes her door.

"You know you can call me if you ever need help, right?"

"I couldn't call anyone. I had to hold still. And then Cujo saw me, so he waited in case I needed help, but I didn't really. I knew what to do. I'm just shaken up because I've never had to actually do it before."

"I'm glad Cujo was there. I just want to be sure you know you can always call me if you need anything."

"Thanks. But I'm okay, really."

"I know."

"Okay. But if you don't stop squeezing my hand so hard, you're going to break my fingers."

"Shit. I'm sorry. I just don't like knowing you could've been hurt." He brings my hand to his mouth and kisses my fingers. "I didn't mean to squeeze so hard."

"I know you wouldn't hurt me on purpose."

"Good. But I wouldn't let anyone else hurt you either. I promise."

"You can't promise something like that. But I appreciate that you'd try."

"I'd die trying, Ivy."

"Well, fortunately for both of us, it's highly unlikely you will ever need to do that."

He holds my door open, and I walk inside, stopping in front of him for a moment. "She didn't die because you didn't try hard enough to protect her."

"I know." He kisses my hand again. "But that's not going to stop me from trying harder with you."

Jensen

Sharing Gifts

Ivy sits in one of my Adirondack chairs, sipping wine and watching the sun start to set while I put fish on the small, open grill behind my casita. "How come you never upgraded that?" she asks.

"I don't know. Once you get used to cooking on it, it's not bad. And it's not like I'm cooking for a whole family."

"What about at the community center? Is there a nicer grill there?"

"No. But there's four of these, so you can cook more at once, just not on the same grill."

"Maybe that can be my gift."

"What gift?"

"After I leave, I want to give something useful to Ivydell. I'll be back to visit, but I want there to be something more than painted signs to show my appreciation for my time here. Petra didn't have to let me come, and nobody had to be nice to me once I got here, but everyone's been great."

"The signs are enough. You don't need to do anything else."

"Well, I'm going to, anyway. I like the grill idea. Where do y'all have stuff delivered when you order it?"

"The few of us who live here year-round use a post office box, but I don't think they'll take delivery of something as big as a grill."

"Hmm, okay. I'll have to buy it at a store, and we can pick it up in your truck. Do you know a good place to go for a grill?"

I flip the fish. "I honestly don't have the first clue."

"Yes, you do. You're a grill guy. I know you know where to buy one." She sits forward in her chair and glares at me. "I am buying one, so you may as well just tell me where to go."

"I'll help you find a place. We can do it after the festival, okay?"

"No, I want to do it before then. Petra said y'all do a big meal together on the Monday night after. That would be the perfect time to break in a new grill."

"We can go buy one on that Monday during the day. That way it'll be a surprise for everybody."

"Why are you being weird about it?"

"I'm not being weird. I've just got a lot to take care of between now and the festival. It makes more sense to do that after."

"How come everything I want to contribute around here gets treated like an afterthought?"

"Okay, now you're just reaching." I take the fish off the grill. "Don't look for a reason to be mad. It's the busiest time of the year. That's all."

"It's been a weird day." She sighs and leans back into her chair.

I think it'll be good for Ivy to have her friend, Zara, here—someone to keep her busy the day before the festival, and to help her process the changes that come on the day after. Ivydell always feels different the Monday after the festival. All the buzzing energy that leads up to the big event is gone. Some people will pack up and leave right away, head off to their next adventure, but some will stay a little longer.

It's funny how things always seem to fall into place here, like there is no bad timing in Ivydell. Things happen when they're meant to happen.

I've been thinking a lot about timing lately, and about the winery plans that I abandoned. It was meant to be a partnership, and I lost my partner. But when I look to the future, I see that biodynamic winery again. My mind reels with new plans and a different place, one that might work out better than my original idea. I see a new way to make it my own.

And more and more, I see a new partner—not for the winery, but for everything.

"Has anyone ever been bitten by a rattlesnake in Ivydell?"

"Not in the four years I've been here."

"Is there any antivenom here?"

"No. Petra says she knows a Native remedy, but she'd just use it to buy time until we could get someone to the hospital."

"I wonder if there are still people who use the old remedy alone."

"Maybe. I'm taking this fish inside. You better follow me if you want to eat."

"So romantic."

"You don't like romance."

"Just checking to see if you were paying attention." She stands and smiles. With the setting sun as a backdrop, it would make a beautiful photograph. But she's no less beautiful when she catches up to me, leaving the sun behind.

I plate the fish with the wild rice she cooked before she went out to look at the sky. She always wants to help, to contribute something.

Ivy

Time Slips Away

I'M TRYING TO GET an early start on my next project for work, but it's like my brain knows it doesn't have to be done yet, so it keeps wandering. I used to like to get a head start on everything. Now, I thrive on finishing at the last minute.

Zara arrives tomorrow. I can't believe it's already Wednesday, but I can't focus on anything except her being here. I'm definitely going to introduce her to everyone first thing. Then I'll show her Ivydell. Maybe we'll go for a drive if she gets here early enough, and I'll take her to that spot where Jensen took me with our picnic from Hilltop. I don't have a truck with a tailgate, but we could sit on my trunk and look out at the view.

We could get the fourth best barbecue in Texas, stop at Hilltop on the way back, and share a few bottles of wine with Myrna.

She has to spend some time with Myrna and see her jewelry. Knowing Zara, she'll want to schedule a session with the Spirit Sisters.

And then Friday, we'll help with any last-minute stuff for the festival.

The slap on my door doesn't even startle me anymore. Josephine flipped her schedule this week so she'd be around for the festival. She and Zara will hit it off for sure. "Open up. We need to talk."

That's not what she usually says. "Hey." I pull the door open so she can step inside. "What's going on?"

"Do not trust April. She's not your friend, Ivy."

"I know you don't like her, Josephine, and I understand why, but she hasn't done anything wrong to me. She's not exactly friendly to anyone as far as I can tell, but—"

"You don't understand anything about her. She has never called me before. Not once. But I heard from her this morning as I was leaving Albuquerque. Said she had to warn me about you."

"What kind of warning?"

"She said she saw you and Cujo hugging on the path, and then you hopped on the back of his bike, wrapped your legs around him, and he drove off toward his casita."

"Josephine, that's not at all what happened, I swear!"

"I know. Cujo had already told me all about your rattlesnake scare. I'm just letting you know that this is the kind of shit she does. Especially where Cujo is concerned, apparently. They should've kicked her out of Ivydell a long time ago. Petra was hoping she wouldn't come back this year after she . . . anyway, just don't make the mistake of trusting her."

"How'd she get your number?"

"From the list."

"What list?"

"We all have each other's contact information."

"Oh. I guess it makes sense that you would." And, of course, it makes sense that I wouldn't have been given the list. I know that, but it doesn't stop me from feeling slighted by it. Every time I turn around, there's one more reminder.

"I can't believe she tried to set me up like that. For the record, the only thing I wrapped around him was my arms, and only to hold on because I was still shaking. Do you think she really believed Cujo and I were sneaking around behind your back?"

"Who knows what goes on in her head? Honestly, she probably just wanted me to freak out on Cujo about it because she knows he hates that kind of shit. Maybe she thought he'd stop seeing me over it. She doesn't get it, though. We're not like that."

"You're the least jealous person I've ever met. How could she have thought that would work with you?"

"Well, you know me a lot better than she does."

I don't know why hearing that makes me feel so much better, but it does. "I'm surprised she didn't call Jensen, too."

"He hung up on her. She pissed me off, but she burned her bridge with Stinger. She better hope she doesn't need anything repaired over the next few weeks."

"Is that how long you think it'll take him to get over it?" I've never seen him truly mad, but I would've guessed he'd hold a grudge longer than a few weeks.

Josephine's mouth opens, but no words come out. Her eyes won't meet mine. She takes a deep breath. "Yeah. I mean, he'll be mad for at least that long. Don't you think?"

"I'm not sure what I think right now." It's not my imagination, dammit. Everybody is acting strange.

"Your friend comes tomorrow, right?"

"She'll get here tomorrow evening. You wanna hang out with us? I was hoping we could drink wine at Myrna's for a while. If Tawny's not too busy, maybe she'll come over, too. I assume the community center will be set up for the festival and off limits."

"Yeah, sure. Are you helping with the final festival prep tomorrow?"

"No one has mentioned anything. I specifically told Petra I wanted to help but she hasn't—"

Josephine and I both laugh at the knock, as if my rising anger has summoned her. I was about to lose it over nothing. Petra steps inside and gives me the rundown. The path needs to be cleaned and raked again, but it'll go much quicker than the first time. All the signs have to be put out—the signs I didn't get a chance to repaint. And since I never got back to her about a casita for Zara, she took it upon herself to prepare the one next to Myrna's.

"When did you do that? I never even saw you over there."

"I came by, but you didn't answer. Assumed you were with Stinger."

"You should've called me. I would've come and taken care of that. But thanks."

"He's been angry enough lately. I didn't want to add to it by taking you away for a few hours."

"Jensen's been angry? When?"

"Angry is probably not the right word. We're all a little off-kilter, I suppose."

"Because of the festival? Does everyone always get anxious like this right before it?"

Josephine shrugs. "Yeah, I think that's probably it. It's such a big undertaking, but you forget every year how draining it is."

"It is draining," Petra agrees. She doesn't seem agitated, and that's weird, too, because someone just answered for her, and she won't usually let that slide. The woman likes to speak for herself.

"Sneaks up on you," Josephine says.

"Sure does. Time slips away. Speaking of Stinger, he's going to be busy all weekend, so if you want to see him again before Monday night's dinner, tonight is probably your last chance. I assume you'll want to spend time with Zara tomorrow night."

"Yeah, I was thinking maybe I'd introduce her to everyone, take her to dinner, and then we could hang out with anyone who's available for a wine night."

"Why the hell not?" Petra throws her arms up. "I don't think it's going to hurt anything if we're all running on adrenaline this year. We can sleep Monday."

"Jensen can't. He and I have an errand to run on Monday."

"Good luck with that," Josephine says.

"Hey," I say, looking directly at Petra. "Did you really just encourage me to spend time with Jensen?"

She smiles. "I must be getting soft in my old age."

"What about packaging your soaps? And we never made the candles. Damn, time really did slip away."

"You can wrap soaps tomorrow until your heart's content. I'll send you home with plenty of oils to make candles. Maybe you can start a side business."

The reality of how short my time here is hits hard. Zara leaves Tuesday morning, and I leave on Friday. Next week is it.

I tell Petra I want to help with all the outside work in the morning, and then I'll wrap her soaps in the afternoon. She waves me off when I tell her I'll be able to help again on Friday. "No way. Zara is driving nine hours to see you. Spend Friday with your friend. The weekend will be over before you know it."

Josephine says she'll be available for whatever needs to be done. Petra thanks us both, and then she leaves.

I try not to read too much into anything, to not let my imagination get carried away.

"Are you a vendor at the festival?" It hadn't occurred to me before to ask Josephine if she was doing tattoos here this weekend, but I assumed she would be.

"No. I'm not an artist this weekend. I'm just a helper."

"I leave next week." I don't know why I say it so abruptly.

"I know."

"What if I changed my mind about getting a tattoo before I left?" Yeah, not sure why I just said that out loud either.

"I'll be around until Thursday." She leaves with a self-assured smile on her face.

I have exactly one week to decide. I text Jensen.

> *Thinking about getting a tattoo.*

> ...

I don't wait for his words to appear.

> *Wondering if you might want to come exam-ine every inch of my body and tell   me where I should get it.*

> *I might have to go over you twice to be sure.*

> *Door is unlocked and I'm already naked.*

I'm a liar, but I can be naked by the time he gets here.
Barely.

"Whoa. Did you drive or take a plane?"

"I was close when you sent the first text. You weren't naked yet when you sent me the last one, though."

"But I am now." I toss my underwear on the bed.

"Hands on the mattress. Bend over." He reaches behind his back and locks my door.

"Ah, starting your inspection with my backside, huh?"

"Sure."

I love when his smile turns devious. His eyes glimmer. He licks his lips, and steps toward me, counting as he advances. "One. Two."

"A countdown? Is that supposed to scare me?" My toes curl in anticipation of his next move. There's a tingling sensation at the base of my spine, making it nearly impossible to stand still.

"Three." He lunges for me.

I yelp, but I don't run away. He laughs, knowing he succeeded in scaring me. I'm braced for him to spin me around or push me onto the bed, but he sinks his hands deep into my hair on either side of my face and stares into my eyes. "You should know that I think of you as mine, Ivy Dell McAdams. I can't tell you when it started, but if knowing this makes you uncomfortable, I need you to tell me. If a relationship isn't what you want, say it now."

"There's no part of me that wants to say that. As long as you know that I'm not going to change for you, Jensen James Stinger. Not one bit. I'm still going to be me, even the parts that make you crazy. If knowing this makes you want to reconsider, you should do that now."

"I've spent the past four years of my life considering and recon-sidering, questioning every choice I ever made, and I have never felt more certain about anything than I do you."

I blink tears from the corners of my eyes. His kiss is soft, and his fingers massage my scalp as his tongue finds mine. I don't do romance, dammit.

He's already changed me. "I guess you want to make love to me now, too."

"Right after I'm done tattooing my handprint on your ass."

And they say the perfect man doesn't exist.

He kisses my neck, and brings his hands to my back, pulling me closer.

"You need to claim me first?"

"I might need to claim you all night long." His warm hands glide up and down my back.

"The last thing I expected to find here was a shirtless man with a scorpion tattoo, who would change my whole life." I trace the scorpion's tail with my fingertip.

"Is that what you tell your friends about me?" He squeezes my ass.

"Of course not. I tell them you're just some hot guy I'm fucking to pass the time."

"Well, they probably need some new material." He pulls the blanket off my bed. "Wrap up."

"Why?"

"So if any cars pass us, they won't realize you're riding in my truck completely naked."

"Where are we going?"

"To a place with an incredible view."

"Sunset's almost over."

"Full moon. I'll be able to see you just fine."

Jensen

Starshine

I'm actually a little shocked that Ivy let me carry her to my truck wrapped in a blanket. No protest even when I fastened her seatbelt for her. She had to readjust to free her arms, but now she's sitting in my passenger seat with a blanket wrapped around her like a towel, as if it's something she always does.

Sometimes, I think I know what's going on in her head, but all I know right now is that she doesn't seem bothered at all. I'm not sure if it's because she trusts me, or if she's five steps ahead of me and I just haven't figured it out yet.

"Where are we going?"

"Somewhere we've been before."

"I'm not going in Hilltop like this."

"Why not? Shane might give you a discount."

"Seriously, Jensen. Where are we going?"

Okay, so she's definitely not five steps ahead of me. She sounds a little worried. This could be fun.

"I already told you. To a place with a view."

The turn is just up ahead. She's going to figure it out any second. Her smile reveals when it hits her. I turn the wheel without saying a word and drive to the spot.

When I reach the overlook and back in, she looks a little worried again. "You plan on us getting out of this truck?"

"No view through the windshield."

"If you turned the truck around, there would be."

"But I'm not turning the truck around." I open my door and get out, walk around the front of the truck as her eyes track me, and open her door.

She bites her bottom lip. Is it anticipation, or is she thinking of resisting? I reach across her body and unhook her seatbelt, slide an arm behind her back, and lift her out of her seat. The way her body softens so I can pick her up sends my dick into the exact opposite state.

I lower the tailgate and set her onto it. She pulls the blanket up over her shoulders and wraps it tightly around her again.

"You know you're not leaving that on, right?"

"I can't take it off out here."

"Why? You were naked in front of me before we left Ivydell."

"Yeah. In front of you but protected by walls and doors. A roof. This is too exposed. Too vulnerable."

"I've seen you naked outside before." I playfully tug on the blanket. "At the circle."

"And then we had to make a run for it because there was a rattlesnake."

"You don't run from rattlesnakes. You hold still. I know you know that." I tug again on the blanket. "Besides, it was only an owl. And we're much closer to the truck this time."

"Someone else could pull in."

"I've been out here hundreds of times and no one ever has."

"Someone could just walk right up. A mountain lion could come along."

"This blanket won't protect you from a mountain lion, but if one happens along, I promise, I will. And nobody is walking around out here. It's just us."

"I can't."

"I'll be right back."

"Where are you going? Don't leave me alone!"

I lean into the truck and connect the audio on my phone, turn up the volume, and go back to her. "There. Now there's music to scare away animals."

"Or attract them."

"The only thing being attracted out here is me to you."

My hands cover hers where she holds the blanket shut. She relaxes her arms and lets me open it, but her body shifts nervously. She's usually so bold. It's one of my favorite things about her, but this? I like this, too. God, she's beautiful.

I push the blanket back and off her shoulders. It falls behind her, and I step between her legs, thread my fingers into her hair on either side of her face and kiss her. I love to hold her face and kiss her like this. She is naturally passionate and playful, but when I initiate this deep kiss, she kisses me back the same way.

When she first stopped resisting or trying to change up this style of kiss, I let myself start thinking she might feel something more than either one of us wanted to acknowledge. I knew I felt it, and I'd missed kissing like this so damn much.

I've never kissed a woman deeper than I felt just to play a role, never let it be performative. Sometimes, I've avoided kissing at all because kisses can mislead, but when they're honest, they can also confirm.

Crickets trill in the near distance. Coyotes howl farther off and likely below, the sound being lifted by the wind. It's a clear night. So much is clear.

I end the kiss and hop up into the bed of the truck. "Slide back. I've got the blanket." She lets me pull her to the center, where I spread out the blanket and lie next to her, propped on my elbow, gazing at her body under the stars.

She smiles up at me. "Are you not taking your clothes off?"

"Not right now." I stroke her cheek and continue down her neck, spreading my palm flat when I reach her chest, holding it there for a moment to warm her cool skin, watching the rise and fall of her breath, the way her nipples look darker in the moonlight while the rest of her skin looks lighter. I trace around a nipple with my fingertip until she squirms on the blanket, bringing my thumb in then to pinch softly and roll it gently as her body stops moving but her breaths quicken.

Moving my hand down her ribcage, I map the contours of her bones and the hollows in between. She shivers slightly when I reach her belly where the protective cage ends and her soft skin isn't stretched so taut, her unguarded center. Pausing again to watch the rise and fall, to feel the way my hand lifts without leaving her body, I marvel at the realness of her. At the unlikeliness of our paths ever crossing.

Leaving my hand on her stomach, I kiss her. Deeply, honestly, and she accepts it and returns it.

I brush her hair off her forehead so I can see every inch of her face. "How the hell did any of this happen?"

"A sad, confused girl from the beach woke up one day, determined to see the weird little pocket of the desert that inspired her name because she thought she'd find all her answers there. So, she ignored the well-intentioned advice against it, hit the road, and came crashing into your life, destroying all your peace and solitude."

"You didn't destroy anything. I don't know if you found any of the answers you needed, but I am so damn glad you found me."

"Me, too. Even if you were a jerk."

"I lit your fireplace."

"You had ulterior motives."

"So did you."

"You totally took advantage of me with your snowy kisses and bare chest."

"You intentionally seduced me with your little half sweater and tight leggings."

"But you kissed me first."

"You kissed me back."

"Kiss me now."

My mouth closes on hers, and my hand drifts lower on her body. She parts her legs as soon as my fingers slide between them. Her pussy is soft and warm, so wet and tight, drawing my fingers inside. She relaxes under the stars, and my thumb circles her clit while her tongue dances with mine.

Mine.

When her pleasure peaks and her eyes flutter behind their lids while her spine arches and the tiny quakes of her muscles reverberate on my hand, it's the most beautiful thing I've ever experienced. It's not an unfamiliar moment, but the full moon and all the scents and sounds of the desert night enhance it, make it unlike any other.

I needed to give her this, something uniquely ours, but just as much, I needed to take it for myself. She sighs and buries her face in my shoulder. I slide my fingers slowly in and out of her as she recovers, ready to get her off a second time as soon as she's ready to go.

"I don't think I can come again," she whispers.

"We're not leaving until you do."

"Who said I wanted to leave? Unzip your pants."

"Not yet. I brought you out here so I could enjoy your naked body."

"I think you might enjoy the way I was planning to use it."

"I'm sure I would, but I haven't figured out where your tattoo should go yet."

"Oh, yeah."

I sit up. "Lay face-down across my lap."

Surprisingly, she does it with no arguing or bargaining. I draw tiny circles to tickle behind her knee, and her legs bends like it's spring-loaded, capturing my fingers. When she straightens it again, I draw a heart.

The corner of her smile is visible through the section of her hair that's fallen across her face. It's not fiery like when sunlight hits it, but it shines for the moon, too. My hand roams up the back of her thigh, squeezing just below the curve over her butt cheek to watch it swell.

I rub over her firm, rounded ass, and I can't resist the urge to spank it a few times. She draws a quick breath at the first slap and holds it, and the sudden silence around us feels like the whole desert follows her lead.

The wind blows over her back, prompting her exhale. I caress the warmth under my hand, and wonder if I've turned her skin red as the crickets start to sing again. My palm glides to the small of her back. Her hips rock, encouraging me to massage her there. When I rub this spot at her lower back, I imagine my hand there, guiding her into a room full of people. Announcing to them all that she is with me. She's mine.

I continue to massage as my hand moves up her back and to her shoulders.

"Roll over."

She looks up at the stars, her eyes shimmering. My hand massages her tits, my thumb brushing over each nipple in turn. Looking over her blank canvas body, I wonder what she'll get if she decides to go through with the tattoo.

The dip just inside her hipbones is one of my favorite spots to kiss. My mouth can't reach it from here, but I kiss the pads of my fingers that were inside her minutes ago, and then press them to the spot to transfer the kiss to her skin. "Right here," I say.

She smiles. "That seems like a tender spot for a tattoo."

"I'll kiss it every night."

Her face falls. "You won't see it every night."

"Every chance I get, I'll kiss it."

"Maybe your kiss should be the tattoo. Did you know lip prints are like fingerprints? You could identify someone by them if you had a reference. Of course, if things didn't work out between us, that would be awkward to explain to the next guy."

"I can't think of a better reason to have my lips tattooed on your body."

"Gross. Don't be that guy."

"Every man is that guy. And no matter what you choose for your tattoo, I want to be the only one who ever gets to kiss it."

She flashes what I know is meant to be a look of disapproval. All

I see is stars shining in the prettiest eyes in the world.

"Spread your legs." I cup her pussy in my hand. "This is mine, and I'm not done playing with it."

The look intensifies, but her legs fall open.

Mine.

But the way I belong to her outweighs all the stars in the sky.

She fucking owns me.

Ivy

Togetherness

LONG BEFORE I FEEL his weight in my bed or hear his snore, I know Jensen is next to me. The amethyst woman staring at me is the surest sign that I am not alone, even before the memories of last night confirm it.

"Good morning," I whisper.

Jensen groggily mumbles a response.

"I was talking to the angel."

"She's not an angel. No wings."

"Maybe angels don't really have wings. Have you ever actually seen one?"

His heavy arm lands on my waist and drags me across the mattress to him. "I'm seeing one right now."

"It's entirely too early for that much cheese." I try to wrestle out of his grasp, but he won't let me go. "Stop. I have to pee."

He reluctantly releases me. I turn the angel around before I climb out of bed.

When I return from the bathroom, the shoulder tattoo Josephine gave him peeks out above the blanket, and the angel is staring at me again. "I keep telling you, you better leave her alone."

"She can't keep her eyes off you," he says, rolling to face me. "Her dark, empty eyes that follow you everywhere you go."

He holds the blanket open, and I climb back into bed with him. His body is warm, and I could fall back asleep in his arms in no time, but I have to go. "I'm helping clean the path again this morning."

"We better warm up your legs." He pulls me on top of him, and I don't resist.

I slide down onto his morning erection and moan. How could I not make that sound at the way he stretches me when I take his dick at this angle? So fucking good. He gave me three orgasms under the stars and the full moon last night. Another after we got back here. I can give him one with no reciprocation this morning.

Rocking back, I ride his cock slowly, going all the way down every time. His eyes are glazed, and I love it when he looks at me like this, but I need to hurry things along. He tries to slow me back down when I start to bounce on him, but I smile and shake my head. "It's gotta be quick and dirty this morning, babe."

"Did you just call me babe? You can do whatever you want now."

"I never knew you wine country boys were so easy."

"Only for beach girls."

"Shut up and let me fuck you."

That appreciative smile is everything. I wish I could take my time, but this day is going to be so busy, and then Zara will be here. She's going to love Jensen. How could anyone not?

Just when I think I'm going to have to push past my difficulty with dirty talk in the daylight and start spitting some filthy shit to get him there, his body tightens and his groans shorten along with his breath. My vampiric inner slut is grateful. So are my quads. I'm tactful enough not to throw up victory arms. But only just.

I kiss his scorpion before I dismount. "What are you doing this morning?"

"Putting out signs."

"No, that's this afternoon. I'm helping with those, and then I'm packaging soap for Petra."

"How many hours are in your day? Because I think you must have more than the rest of us."

I toss a towel at him, aiming for his chest, but hitting his face. "Don't do the signs without me."

"You better get your ass in gear if you're working with me this morning."

"Pffft. I'll work circles around you." I send Petra a text to let know I'm helping with the signs this morning unless she needs me somewhere else. She says that's fine. Everything's covered.

I HAD NO IDEA driving metal pickets into the ground would be this hard. We've been at it for hours and we're not close to being done. The warning signs for the path are still stacked in the bed of Jensen's truck and we've got two more rows of the other signs to put out before we can even start on those.

Hearing from Zara rejuvenates me.

The first four hours of the drive are done. Just got gas and I'm about to get back on the road. I think I'm past all the major traffic areas now. The rest should be smooth sailing.

I tried to tell her to fly, but I'm glad she's almost halfway here.

Cujo shows up to help with the signs and Jensen tells me to take off.

"Are you firing me?"

"I'm offering you the chance to get out of the sun and wind and go wrap bars of soap."

"You're fired," Cujo says. "There. Now you have no choice."

It feels amazing to take off the work gloves Jensen loaned me. They probably saved my hands from blisters, but they're hot. I open and close my fingers, let the wind blow through them. "Fine. I'm out of here."

Petra's casita is cool and quiet. I yawn as I look over all the supplies that she laid out for me. It is too early to be this tired. I've got a late night ahead, catching up with Zara, and then showing her all around tomorrow and the festival all weekend.

I wrap twine around a bar of soap to measure the length I'll need with the bow, and then I cut a pile the same length. For the wax paper, I can eyeball the amount without precutting. That can vary a little. There's a pair of scissors and a bowl of dried herbs to cut trimmings from for decoration, and a stack of paper with a couple of pens for making the labels. As long as I keep my hands busy, I should be able to stay awake.

Separating the soap by scent, I do the labels first, using the scissors to make a hole big enough to push the twine through. Then I cut coordinating herb sprigs and group everything to make the wrapping go faster. It only takes a few hours to have them all done.

Zara should be on the home stretch. Just a few more hours. I walk back to my casita, stopping to pet Wizard on the way. "You didn't leave any new gifts on my porch, did you?"

April's shadow darkens my mood. It worsens when I look up to see her face. "What do you want?" I ask.

"My cat."

"Does it look like I'm holding him hostage?"

"Maybe things aren't always what they look like."

"Really? You figure that out all by yourself?" I give Wizard a final neck rub, and stand.

"What was I supposed to think?"

"Maybe you weren't supposed to think anything at all. Maybe it was none of your business. But if you were just dying to know, you could've asked instead of jumping to conclusions. Josephine and I are friends, and I'd thought maybe I could be friends with you, too. What were you hoping to accomplish by telling her that, anyway?"

"I don't know. It just looked like you were one more woman he wanted instead of me, and it pissed me off."

"You don't get to shit on other people's lives just because your feelings are hurt. Cujo and Jensen are friends. No matter what you thought about me, did you really think he'd do that?"

"I didn't think, okay? I just got hurt and reacted."

"Overreacted."

"That's fair. I'm sorry."

Well, damn. I wasn't expecting an apology. "Just cut it the fuck out, okay? Don't try to start any more rumors about me."

"Why is someone coming to visit you?"

"How do you know that?"

"There are no secrets in Ivydell."

"She's a good friend, and she's dying to see Ivydell for herself. It's honestly more her kind of place than it is mine. So, I invited her to come."

"Might as well show it to people while you can."

"Exactly. I don't have much time left."

"And then what?"

"And then I go home."

"What about Stinger?"

"For some strange reason, I don't feel compelled to confide in you, April."

"Got it. I'll just take my cat and be on my way then."

I step aside, not that I'm preventing Wizard from going any-where, no matter where I stand. April turns around and starts walking away. "Come on, Wizard."

The cat pads along behind her, his fluffy tail swishing as he goes. Such a good boy. So loyal. If that cat loves her so much, she can't be terrible.

I hear Myrna's laugh coming from the direction of the path, so I detour that way. Tawny and Josephine are helping, too.

"How close is your friend?" Petra asks.

"Just a few more hours. Is the community center off limits tonight? I was thinking we could do another girls' night, and it might be better to do it there than at someone's casita. More space."

Less chance of Josephine kicking the shit out of April, assuming they'd both come.

"Fine with me," Petra says. Tawny and Myrna agree, both say they'll be there.

Josephine looks up from the rake she's wielding. "I'll let Alma and Elma know."

"Thanks." She knows I'm still a little uncomfortable approaching Whispering Winds. I like the Spirit Sisters, but their casita makes me antsy.

"Y'all need any help out here?"

"Nope." I swear they all say it in unison. I'd be offended if I didn't know they were trying to be nice.

"Okay, fine."

I walk to April's casita, take a deep breath, and knock on the door. She eyes me warily when she opens it. "Girls' night at the community center tonight. I want to introduce my friend, Zara, to everyone. You should come."

"Maybe I will."

"See you there."

Jensen calls to say they're done with the signs, and he and Cujo are going to pick up barbecue for an impromptu community dinner. "Should I get wine, too?"

"Yes, please. It was planning to host girls' night, but I guess now it's a unisex party. You're saving me from having to go to the store."

He laughs. "Were you planning to include all the girls?"

"I've invited them all."

"Are they all aware?"

"We're all adults. I'm sure it'll be fine."

"Your optimism is boundless."

"It's Ivydell. No one should be excluded here."

I hear him filling Cujo in on my plans for the night as we're ending our call—and Cujo's gravelly voice saying, "Your old lady's fearless."

Not loving the *old lady* bit. But I kind of like the fearless part. I used to fear so many pointless things. The desert changes people.

Petra

Through the Hourglass

I STARE AT THE woman in the mirror and wonder how she got here. Her hair should be longer and darker, her skin smoother, and her convictions less wavering.

I'm not so tough anymore, Patty. Tonight is the last time that what's left of Ivydell will come together before the festival. This festival being Ivy's first. Ironic, no? You probably wouldn't think so. You'd say it was exactly how it was meant to be. I'd call bullshit, even though a part of me would believe you. I believe a little more in the timing of the universe now. There's no denying that I'm done trying to hold back the wind, huh?

I laugh at my reflection, but it's not entirely self-deprecating. Hell, I'm happier than I've been since I don't know when. Looking around me, I see people I care for finding happiness. And that's got to count for something. In the end, this wasn't all for nothing. I've got to believe it was always supposed to be this way.

It mattered that we were here. We made a difference. Changed some people's lives.

Healed a few hearts. Maybe even one that didn't deserve it.

I'm grateful. Just so goddamn grateful for it all.

Jensen

Not the Time or Place

CUJO AND I HANG out and have a few beers while we wait for our large to-go order. We could've called it in to be ready when we got here, but it's better this way. My shoulders are sore, but my body feels light. There is a lot of work ahead for the weekend, but I'm neither dreading nor looking forward to it. It'll be what it'll be. And it'll be all right.

"What are your immediate plans?" I ask.

"Gonna eat some barbecue, drink a few more beers, might sing a few songs before the night's over."

"You, asshole. You know I didn't mean for tonight."

"Well, I'm not in the mood to talk about the future beyond tonight."

"Understood."

"Looks like I'm going to have to ask Jojo to give me a tattoo."

"Yeah, I may have heard something about that."

"I bet you did."

"She's just trying to help. She wants everybody to be happy."

"I don't know how she went this long never seeing the place she was named for, but she had no trouble fitting in."

"My best guess would be that Ivy could fit in just about any-where."

"You've got that in common then," he says, shaking his head.

"You think?"

"I know. When your ass showed up, I told Petra you didn't belong in Ivydell. You belonged on a golf course. She told me I didn't know what the hell I was talking about." He laughs his big rolling laugh. "She might've been right."

"I'm glad you decided to give me a chance."

"So am I, brother. You turned out all right."

"You think I'm finally grown, huh?"

"I think you might be about ready to fly."

By the time we get to the community center with barbecue, beer, and wine, the party has already kicked off. Everybody's showered and changed. I help drop off the food and booze, and then I slip back out to get myself cleaned up. Ivy's friend will be here soon, and for the first time in a very long time, I actually care about making a good first impression on somebody.

Cujo and I walk out together. "Full moon," he says, looking up at the sky.

"My favorite phase." I smile thinking about Ivy in the bed of my truck last night.

We head in opposite directions to get cleaned up, but we're both doing it for a girl. I'm the only one who will admit it, but he's not fooling me. It might be true that he and Josephine don't want anything serious, but they're pretty serious about what they've got. For now, anyway.

Ivy's red hair is the first thing I see when I walk back into the party. It bounces as she pulls Zara along to introduce her to someone else. She leans in closer to her friend to say something, and they both smile. Her eyes light up when she spots me, and I don't have to see mine to know they've had the same reaction.

I walk to her like I'm being pulled on a cable.

"Zara, this is Jensen."

"It's a pleasure," I say. "I've heard a lot about you."

"Probably not as much as I've heard about you." She turns to Ivy. "You said he didn't own a shirt."

I roll my eyes as they laugh. "I rented this one just for tonight. Don't spill anything on me. I'll lose my deposit."

Josephine joins us. "Hi, you must be Zara. I'm Josephine."

"You're the tattoo artist! I saw you on that show. As soon as Ivy told me about you, I knew who you were."

"I can't believe you watched it. And that you remember it."

"Listen, I thought my friend ran off to live with a bunch of hermits. Then she tells me she has a celebrity for a next-door neighbor!"

Josephine blushes, and I don't think I've ever seen that from her. I forget she was on a TV show. She's so humble, but I know she's a big name in her industry. Cujo says she'll always try to downplay it, even with him.

He walks up behind her now with a proud smile on his face.

Zara looks like she wants to say something, but she's nervous.

Ivy nods at her, and she says, "I know this weekend is going to be really busy, but if you have any time, I'd love to talk to you about a tattoo I've been wanting for a while. If it's something you'd be interested in doing, I'll book an appointment and fly out to your studio."

"You don't have to do that. I can do it while you're here."

Cujo's eyebrows lift. "Huh, how long have I known you now? And you haven't offered to tattoo me in Ivydell." He smiles at Zara. "You must make a better first impression."

"Wait," Josephine says. "You never asked. I didn't know you wanted me to."

Ivy was right. She definitely wants to give him a tattoo. Her whole face is glowing.

"Okay, look," she says. "I'm here all weekend. I'll be more than happy to tattoo all three of you."

Zara and Cujo nod and smile. Ivy doesn't look as excited, but she is smiling. I think she might go through with it. She blows me a kiss.

We all sit together and eat. Everyone is running on the same buzzing energy that always precedes the festival. In so many ways, this feels like every year since I've been here, but it'll be different. Smaller can be good sometimes.

"I can't believe I have my own casita," Zara says. "I feel so special."

"I'll be right next-door if you need anything, doll," Myrna says. She's come over to introduce herself. And, of course, she's wearing her signature pendant. Her logo.

I'm sure Ivy warned Zara about Wild Love, but it would be hard not stare even if you were expecting it. "I'd love to see all your jewelry."

"Come over in the morning. I'll be polishing everything and putting my displays together."

April walks in, and Ivy waves.

Josephine sucks in a breath, but she doesn't say a word. Cujo puts his arm around her.

Wise move. Sends a clear message to April, and hopefully, calms Josephine. She may not have left at the sight of her, but it's obvious she's not thrilled about April being here, either.

Petra goes over and leads April to the food, chatting as they walk. We just might make it through this party with no drama. There's never been much drama in Ivydell at all, but April can't seem to help herself sometimes.

"We've got homemade cookies for dessert," Tawny yells from the counter.

"When did she have time to bake?" Ivy asks.

I refill her wine glass. "If she's not painting, she's baking."

"She and I each managed to get several dozen baked today in between chores," Myrna says. "There's plenty so eat up."

"Anybody else need more wine?"

Zara holds up her glass.

Shadow and Dice come in together, both carrying guitar cases. I see Cujo's already leaning against the wall in the corner. They place theirs next to his before they head for the barbecue. I'm glad they're going to play tonight. It's one of the things I'll miss most about this place.

I see Ivy and Zara walk away from the corner of my eye. They stop to talk to the resident mediums. She said Zara would be fascinated by the spooky sisters, and I can see by the look on her face that she is.

Dice comes over after he and Shadow find a place to set their plates. He kneels down between me and Cujo at the end of the table.

"You get anything out of him?" Cujo asks.

"Yeah," Dice nods. "He's going to be fine. Probably got more solid plans than most of us."

"Good." I'm relieved. Shadow's the oldest resident in Ivydell. I'd hate to leave not knowing that everyone was doing okay, especially him.

"And I hear you've got grapevines dancing in your eyes," Dice says. "Going back to your roots?"

"In my own way. On my own terms."

"The only way to do anything worth doing." He stands, nodding at Cujo. "I better go eat before this crooner decides he needs backup."

"You better eat fast," Cujo says.

This conversation needs to wrap up before Ivy comes back, anyway. I haven't shared my plans with her yet. This isn't the time or the place. We'll talk before she leaves.

Ivy
Somebody Had to Say It

THE LOOK ON ZARA's face when Cujo starts to sing must be the exact expression of shock I had the first time I heard his voice. Josephine watches him with that awestruck gaze she always gets when he's singing.

"Good wine, homemade cookies, and live music." Zara smiles. "And it's only the first night. I can't wait to see what the rest of the weekend brings."

"Same," I say. "I'm super excited to see how the festival goes. And for you to see the prairie dogs. And the chipmunks!"

"As long as I don't see any mountain lions or rattlesnakes."

"Don't forget about the scorpions. You don't want to meet one of those either."

"Shit. I forgot about those. I'm never taking my shoes off here."

"Good plan."

The guys put down their guitars, and Cujo says he needs to soothe his vocal cords, which just means he wants another beer. I think he mostly wants to put his arms around Josephine. He goes straight to her and wraps her up like he hasn't seen her in days, but he's been staring at her all night long.

Dice pretends he came over to talk to Jensen, but he's too transparent. All he really wants to do is hit on Zara. He's a little old for her, if you ask me, but she hasn't asked me, and she hasn't exactly shut him down either. I don't know his actual age, so maybe I'm overestimating it. Maybe she doesn't care.

She's very intrigued that someone could actually play poker for a living. For all I know, he might be her perfect type. Dice isn't a bad looking man, but I wouldn't call him conventionally attractive. He's got that weird sex appeal of celebrity chefs and aging rock stars—strong features, bold confidence, makes it clear he doesn't give a shit how anybody else thinks he's supposed to live.

I get it in a way, but I've always been more drawn to the quietly confident type. At any rate, I never would've put Dice and Zara together. Not that they're together, but it's also only the first night. When he walks off to go to the bathroom, Zara leans in and asks, "He's really single, right?"

But she's not asking me. She's looking right at Jensen. "Yeah," he says. "Divorced."

"Hmmm," is all she says.

Guess it's a good thing she has her own casita after all. Of course, Dice has his own, too. I have a feeling I might not see her much after the sun goes down this weekend.

Maybe there truly is something in the air in Ivydell.

Josephine and Cujo come over to join our conversation when Dice returns. Petra follows, and then Myrna. Before long, Tawny and Leo make their way into the circle, and we're all huddled up with conversations weaving and spinning. The Spirit Sisters mostly listen, but I can't be sure if they're hearing us or voices that the rest of us don't detect. Even April contributes without agitating anyone.

Petra says the group may be smaller this year, but it has some of the best people Ivydell has ever known.

Leo declares it's going to be the best festival they've ever had.

Shadow says he's sure glad to be here for it, which strikes me as funny because Jensen has told me Shadow hates the festival.

Zara says she can't wait to see Ivydell during the day. Dice leans down and says something meant for her ears only, but I'm standing close enough to catch something about the way he wants to see her tonight. My brain nopes out on that as quickly as possible, and I put a few more inches between us. We're all adults, but they can keep their private talk private.

"I'm going to miss this place so much," I say. "I'm not even gone yet, and I already can't wait to come back."

"Why would you come back?" April says. "Surely you could see a windfarm closer to home."

"What?"

Everyone talks at once, rapid-fire words, obviously meant to distract me, or to drown out April's response.

"What do you mean about a windfarm?" I ask, raising my voice.

They all stop talking and glare daggers at April.

"Why?" Myrna goes up onto the toes of her red snakeskin ankle boots to make eye contact with her. "Why!"

"Damn you, April." Petra shakes her head.

In April's defense, she looks genuinely stunned. But I still don't know what the hell is happening. "Tell me what you meant."

She looks at the floor in silence.

Jensen's hand meets the small of my back. "This is it, Ivy. The last year for the festival."

"Why?"

Petra closes her eyes like she's summoning strength. When she opens them, she says, "Because none of us will be here next year. You leave next week, and over the following month, we will all do the same."

"But why?"

Jensen moves his hand to my hip. "Because the women who own Ivydell have sold it, which was the exact right thing for them to do. It was time."

"No! Let's talk to them. You have to fight. Y'all did it once. And you won!"

"But we don't want to fight anymore, doll." Myrna's voice is soft.

"Jensen speaks the truth, Ivy." Alma sighs. "It was time."

"Who are these women?"

Petra steps forward. And then Myrna. Alma and Elma fall in line next to them.

"The four of you own Ivydell?"

"Well, doll," Myrna begins. "When we won the right to come back, someone had to start paying the taxes. It was abandoned land when Ivydell was originally settled, and it sat under the radar for nearly sixty-five years until that oil and gas company took notice. Before that, it was just a patch of worthless land nobody else cared about, but by fighting over it, we declared it had worth, so someone had to take legal ownership."

"The four of you stepped up and took it on." I'm in awe. It should've occurred to me that someone had to own Ivydell. It's not really an autonomous magical realm in the middle of the desert. It's land, and land has value. I understand that. But I don't understand this.

"Is it really going to be turned into a windfarm?"

Petra laughs. "God, how I wish your Gran was here to give her perspective on this, complete with all her wind metaphors. There were so many signs that we were doing the right thing. But somehow, when you reached out to ask if you could come and see Ivydell, I finally stopped questioning it. Knowing you were coming to see it, to experience this place Patty loved, it closed the circle for me. I knew we'd made the right decision."

"You knew this was happening before I even came?"

"These things take time."

I look around at these faces I've come to consider friends. "Did everyone know? Everyone except me?"

"Ivy." Jensen's tone is stern and condescending, and I hate him for it.

Spinning to step out of his reach, I turn toward him. "You knew. This whole time, you fucking lied to me."

"I have never lied to you."

"A lie of omission is still a lie. If you can justify that, maybe I don't know you at all. What else would keep from me and feel totally fine about?"

The circle widens as everyone begins to step away. Cujo holds Josephine's shoulders when she stops and refuses to move. She glares at April. "You miserable bitch. You just can't stand for anyone to enjoy a single goddamn happy moment, can you?"

"I didn't mean to tell her, but someone should've done it a long time ago. It wasn't right to keep her in the dark."

"Don't you dare," Petra warns. "Don't you dare try to justify it. And I'll be damned if I'll let you stand here and make yourself out to be her friend."

"Was anyone else ever going to tell me?"

"Of course," Jensen says.

"I was going to come and tell you in person," Petra says.

"Come where? To the beach? You were going to let me leave, knowing I planned to come back and visit? Let me believe I could be a part of Ivydell forever, and not tell me it was ending?"

"Oh, sweet girl," Elma says. "You are a part of it, but no place on earth lasts forever."

"You weren't going to tell me before I left either." I stare into Jensen's eyes.

"It was Petra's right to tell you, but I had hoped to be there."

"You're a coward."

"I'm going to let that go because I know you don't really believe that about me."

"How am I supposed to know what to believe? This makes me question if I could ever trust you, I know that."

His face is crestfallen. He's hurt, but I really don't trust him right now. My truth may have hurt him, but I'm hurt because he withheld the truth. He knows that the truth is what I came here to find. I came searching for answers. And he just let me be deceived.

Oh, damn. Zara. She didn't drive all day for this shit. "I'm so sorry. You should stay. Enjoy it. All of it."

I run out of the community center because I can't take another second of the sympathetic looks beaming at me from every direction. I don't stop until I reach my casita. Zara walks through my door five minutes later. Jensen is right behind her.

"Zara, I don't know what to say. I feel so bad that you came all this way."

"What do you think you're doing?" she asks.

"I can't stay here. I have to go."

"The hell you do. First of all, you've had too much wine to drive, so that's not happening. Second of all, you're too emotional right now to make decisions about anything. Third of all, I'm so damn glad I was here. I'm here, Ivy."

Tears flow down my cheeks. "It wasn't supposed to be like this."

"I know." She hugs me tight. "But running away won't make it better. Running never helps."

"She's right," Jensen says. "Can I have a few minutes alone with—"

"Tomorrow," Zara says, cutting him off. "You can talk to her tomorrow. I've got her. She's not going to go anywhere, but you need to go."

I won't look at him. I'm grateful she's telling him to go. It's the right thing, and I hate knowing that if I look at him, I might want him to stay. How can any part of me want him right now?

"I'm staying here tonight," she says.

"I'm so sorry, Ivy." I can hear it in his voice. He never meant to hurt me. "But if I had it to do over again, I still wouldn't tell you."

I push Zara away. "Why? How could you treat me like that, knowing I'd end up hurt?"

"Do you know how many people here are hurt because Ivydell is ending? How much bigger the loss is for them than it is for you? Or for me? Those women rebuilt Ivydell. They fought for it, not just for themselves, but for everyone they knew needed this place. But it's time for it to end. And they deserve to be able to let it go without any of us guilting them over it. You can be mad at me for as long as you need to, but don't leave here mad at Petra. Don't shut her out, Ivy. She's the strongest woman I've ever known, but I think that might break her."

"Just go, Jensen."

He walks out, closing the door gently behind him. But he storms right back in before I can take my next breath.

"The reason I would keep it from you all over again is because of the way your eyes lit up when you watched snowflakes coming down. The squeal you let out when you saw your first prairie dog. Your ridiculous anticipation about seeing chipmunks. Because a meteor shower was more to you than falling debris. It was all magical in your eyes, and I told myself you deserved a little magic in your life. But the truth is, it was easy for me not to tell you. Because I desperately wanted to see the world through your eyes. And if I had it to do all over again, I'd make the same selfish choice. I'd choose to let you believe in magic every time. If that makes me a coward, then I guess I am one."

He walks out again, but this time, he doesn't come back.

"What an asshole," Zara says.

"He's the worst man I've ever met."

We both laugh as I fall into her arms.

Petra

Not Done Yet

I DON'T NEED ANOTHER reminder that she's Patty's granddaughter, but if I did, these names she's given my soap scents would solidify the fact. She gave the same scents more than one name, and I don't even have to ask her why. I already know it's so it looks like I have more variety available.

If you tell someone they're smelling Mystic Mint, and then hand them another bar of the same scent but tell them it's Mint Motivation, some people will detect something different and believe they are two distinct formulas. If they didn't like the first one, they might like the second. Smart girl.

Patty never attached a name to her paintings, but she always had a few in mind for each piece. If someone asked if it had a name, she'd tell them the one she felt would resonate most. She didn't do it to mislead anyone. She did it because she wanted people to feel connected to art. To each other. The world around them. Anytime she thought she could provide a connection, there was no stopping her from trying.

"I hope it's okay that I gave them names."

"You sneak up on people as well as your Gran, too."

"You feel safe leaving your door wide open? You're not worried about an animal coming in?"

"Never even thought about it."

"I'm envious. I worry about everything."

"I know you do."

"Can I come in?"

"You never have to ask."

"Why wouldn't she come back, Petra? She hardly went a day without talking about this place. But she didn't even tell us coming back was an option. Why?"

"She'd moved on, hon. She didn't need Ivydell, anymore."

"But she didn't move on. She never found anyone else."

"People can move on alone."

"But we're not supposed to be alone. We're supposed to find our person."

"I'd like to think she did. But her person just wasn't ready for her. And she wasn't really alone. She had you and your mom. And I'm sure she had friends."

"She did. But I wish she could've found love outside of family and friends."

"Again, I'd like to think she did."

"I'm sorry. I didn't mean to insinuate you didn't love each other. It's just that if she wasn't going to come back here for you, why didn't she try to find a new love?"

"I can't answer that. Maybe she did try."

"Did you?"

"I was here. Not a lot of options for me."

"Why didn't you come visit? Why didn't you come after her?"

"I grew and changed, and I knew she did, too."

"You're giving me the old *we loved each other but we weren't in love, anymore* reason?"

"It wouldn't be such a well-known saying if it weren't true for so many people."

"I just hate thinking that she might've died unfulfilled."

"Then stop thinking it. I told you I talked to her before she got too bad to speak."

"Did you ask her why she didn't come back?"

"No. That wasn't the answer I needed. I asked her if she was at peace. She said she'd had a beautiful life." I swipe at my eyes. "Thanked me for being a part of it. And before we hung up, she said, 'Yes, Petra. I am at peace with everything.'"

"You believed her?"

"With all my heart."

"I don't know why I was so convinced there was some big secret I never knew about her life."

I raise my eyebrows and stare at her.

Ivy laughs.

"She didn't necessarily hide that she was a lesbian. I just didn't see it."

"Sometimes, when we lose someone, we fear that their life wasn't big enough, that they missed out on too much. Maybe even start to think that we held them back. Her life was enough, Ivy. She was fulfilled. Are you?"

"No. And I don't think I knew that until I came here."

"That's an important realization. I'm glad you get to take that back with you. We can't fix a problem until we know about it."

"What if I don't know how to be fulfilled?"

"What if you stopped worrying about that and followed your heart?"

"You mean Jensen?"

"If that works out, it'll fulfill a part of your life. But I meant you. What's in your heart for you?"

"That question scares the shit out of me because I've been feeling a strong desire to upend my whole life. Quit my job. Take big risks. And I'm not a big risktaker."

"You haven't *been* a big risktaker. But what I'm hearing is you might be becoming more of one."

"I think you're supposed to tell me not to quit my job. Remind me about health insurance and paid sick days."

"Do I look like someone who has ever had a paid sick day in her life?"

She laughs, and even if my advice is terrible, I'm going to let myself believe I said something right, because the sorrow that veiled her eyes when she walked in has lifted.

"So, do you have something fun planned for you and Zara today?"

"Dice stole her from me at eight a.m.!"

I belly laugh at her incensed response. I'm sure Dice has his own motives, but I think he may have been trying to free Ivy up for Stinger, too. "Well, damn. I guess Ivydell is determined to work a little more magic before we shut her down."

Jensen

Fishing for Forgiveness

Ivy's either not home or she's in a deep sleep in there. I've been banging around at her front door for twenty minutes.

The drill gets her attention. She flings her door open. "What the hell are you doing out here?"

She's been asleep. Her hair is a sexy mess. But her swollen eyes make me want to hold her and apologize until she accepts it. She opens her eyes wide and gestures at the barrier between us. "What is this?"

"It's a screen door."

"How'd you know I wanted a screen door?"

"My mom always like slamming one when she was mad, and this one was just taking up space in my shop, so I figured you could put it to good use." I open the screen door and slam it, mentally patting myself on the back for the good job I did hanging it.

"I'm only going to be here for another week."

"Yeah, well, I might not be done pissing you off yet."

"I'm pretty pissed off that you woke me up."

"Sleeping all day is unhealthy. And rude. Zara came all this way to see you, and you're not even hanging out with her."

"She left me for Dice. And I don't even where they went."

I laugh because I already knew that. "They're fishing with Cujo and Josephine."

"You never took me fishing."

"How come I didn't know you liked to fish?"

"Probably because you never asked."

"Well, damn!" I open her screen door and slam it again.

She bites her lip, trying not to smile. "Does this thing have a latch so the wind won't grab it and bang it open and shut all day and night?"

"No. But if you're nice to me, I could probably find you a latch for it."

"I got a whole door without being nice to you at all."

"That's not true. You just haven't been nice to me today."

"I don't have enough reward points built up from my past nice moments?"

"You might. I guess I could find you a latch based on that."

"You're going to give in, just like that?"

"Would a latch for this door make you happy?"

"You can't just do things because they'll make me happy."

"Try me." I lean my forehead against the screen. "Do you want to go fishing?"

"I'm not sure. Are you going to keep any pertinent information from me?"

"I am going to tell you everything there is to tell about this fishing hole. I am going to describe every lure to you, sparing no details. When you catch a fish, I'm going to count its scales so you'll never have to wonder how many it had. If we—"

"Keep going and you're going to piss me off all over again."

"You got a door for that." I take a few steps back.

She swings it open, and pulls it halfway back before she releases it to let it slam. "Damn, that is pretty satisfying." She slams it again.

I step close enough to press my face back into the screen and pucker my lips against it.

"I am not kissing you through that dirty screen."

"Well, if you're not willing to get dirty, I don't know if I want to take you fishing after all."

"Don't you have work to do?"

"Nothing that's more important than working on us."

"Dammit, quit being great. I'm not ready to forgive you yet."

"You don't have to forgive me yet, Ivy. Just put some shoes on. Let's go fishing with friends."

She slams her new screen door as we leave.

We'll hardly see each other over the next two days. She might forgive me by Monday or she might be completely over me by then, but she's willing to get in the truck with me now, so I'm taking her fishing.

Ivy
Naming Rights

"Everybody keeps saying the festival will be smaller this year," Josephine says as she bounces her line in the water. Cujo grabs her pole and holds it still. He's told her to quit jiggling it a dozen times, but she keeps doing it. "But fewer artists don't mean fewer people will come."

"It won't take them as long to see everything, though," Jensen says.

Dice helps Zara reel in her fourth fish. She's the only one who has caught anything so far. I don't think she really needs his help, but she lets him do it. While he's taking her fish off the hook, she asks if I'm okay.

"I'm good. Or I will be. Did I tell you my mom has a boyfriend?"

"I already knew that. I've seen her out with him."

"I'm glad he takes her to do things. She needs to get out and have fun more often."

"He seems nice. Definite silver fox."

"Really? I haven't seen a picture of him. All I know is he's a doctor. I should've asked her more questions. She probably thinks I don't care."

"I doubt she thinks that. Hasn't she had boyfriends before?"

"Not in a really long time. She dates, but no relationships."

"I think Dr. Daddy might be changing that."

"Do not call him that."

"You'll see."

"So," Josephine says. "I think tonight feels like a good night for tattoos."

"I'm game." Zara nods at Cujo. "You can go first. I guess you outrank me."

"I don't know about all that." He winks at Josephine.

"Actually, I think I should go first. I'm the most likely to back out, so it makes sense to get mine done before I watch someone else and change my mind."

They all look at me like I might be joking. I'm not.

"What did you decide on?" Josephine reels her line back in. It's empty, but she doesn't seem to care about catching anything. Apparently, the only time she can hold still is when she's giving a tattoo. She dances while she's driving, bounces while she's fishing . . .

"I don't know yet."

"But you'll know by tonight?" Josephine asks.

"Yeah, I'll know by then."

Zara rides back to Ivydell with Dice, but we all meet at Vintage Vibes to eat dinner together. It feels almost wrong to eat dinner together at Jensen's casita without inviting everyone else. But a lot of things feel strange here now.

There's an expiration date on Ivydell for everyone, not just me.

I wanted the same status as all the regular residents, and now I've got it. We're all temporary.

We're eating outside on a long folding table that Jensen brought over from the shop. A shooting star adds a flash of magic to the sky.

"I'm going to take the sign for Sparrow's Song," I say. "Not sure what I'll do with it yet, but I want it."

"You can't," Jensen says. "I've already claimed it. I'm taking most of the casita signs."

"For what?"

"I was going to wait until we were alone to tell you my plans, but I don't want you to think I'm keeping it a secret from you. I'm opening a winery."

"Here? Or are you going back to California?" I try not to sound worried that his answer might be the latter, but I don't want him to go farther away. I'm still a little mad at him, and I don't know when it will fully fade, but I'd rather be pissed off at a closer distance. I'd rather be closer, period.

"Neither. Found some options a little closer to the beach. We'd still be a few hours apart, but closer."

"You can't make business decisions based on me."

"It's a good area. Already known for wineries. The fact that it's closer to you is a bonus."

I'm not sure if he's telling the whole truth, but I'm happy for him to finally be following this dream. "Do you have a name?"

"I do. Desert Ivy Vineyards."

"You can't name your winery after me, Jensen."

"I can, actually. I can name it anything I want."

"Ivy doesn't even grow in the desert."

"Yeah, she did."

Our friends all freeze and stare at us. I don't have to make eye contact with any of them to know they think this is some grand romantic gesture, and the line he just said is poetic. It is. But I don't feel swept away by any of it. I might not be sweepable, though.

He's right that I've grown since we met. The woman I was when I got here wouldn't even be speaking to him yet. I'd be having an angry pity party for myself in my casita. Actually, if he hadn't woken me up with that damn drill, I might be doing that. I'm glad I'm not. I'd rather be here.

"Anyway," he says. "It's not like I'm naming it the Ivy Dell McAdams Winery."

"True. At least you didn't go that far. But there's no desert a few hours from me, so it's going to be an odd name for the area."

"Based on the names of some of the other wineries in the area, I'm not worried about mine."

"I still don't see why you need the signs."

"Figured I'd call the tasting room Vintage Vibes. The sign will be a nice touch out in front of it. It'll bring back good memories for me when I see it."

"That's actually a better name for the winery itself. Vintage is a wine term." I don't know why I feel the need to tell him this as if he doesn't know. "Unless it's too casual for what you had in mind overall."

"Formal is the furthest thing from my vision. Maybe Vintage Vibes is a better name. Guess I'd have to drop Vineyards. That might be too much alliteration."

"Yeah. Vintage Vibes is enough. You don't really have to declare the vineyards."

"And that means I can use Ivy in the wine names. I could name my first two releases Wild Ivy and Desert Ivy. I like it."

"You don't have to include Ivy at all."

"But I want her included."

I realize our friends are all still staring at us, watching this very personal conversation unfold. "If you insist on naming a wine after me, you could at least call it Classy Slut."

"I'll put that on a t-shirt."

Everyone laughs. Wolves howl. They're far away, but the wind carries the sound. It can fool you, make you think they're closer.

"Why do you need the Sparrow's Song sign?"

"Everything's not about need. Sometimes, you just want something."

"Well, I want that one."

"I already called dibs."

"If you had a screen door, I'd slam it."

"I'll put one in for you at the winery. We'll call it the Ivy Slammer."

Everybody laughs again. An owl lifts off from the roof. It's too high to touch us, but we all duck a bit when we hear the rush of its unseen wings.

Some things are inherently scary, even when you know there's probably no danger.

Jensen

All About Trust

I was shocked when Ivy offered to be the first one to be tattooed tonight, but I'm even more shocked that she's going through with it.

"Okay," Josephine says. "Moment of truth. Where are we doing it?"

Ivy points to my favorite kissing spot, just inside her hip bone.

"Ooh, how intimate," Josephine teases. "And what am I putting there?"

"A cactus blossom. Looks like they might not bloom before I have to leave. The one I love in Tawny's painting may the only one I get to see, and I don't think I can buy it. I might need to be more conservative with my money for a while. Yellow."

"I love it. Just the flower or do you want it on a cactus? A vignette, maybe?"

"No. Just the flower."

"Take off your pants and let's do this."

Ivy hesitates. I know she hadn't considered that she'd have to take off her pants. For as uninhibited as she is in private, she's not about to strip down to her underwear in front of Dice and Cujo. I open a drawer and take out a pair of pajama pants with a drawstring waist. "Here. These should work."

"Thanks." She goes to my bathroom to change.

"For a girl who grew up in a bikini, she's awfully shy about her body," Josephine says as she sets up her tray.

"She's a time and place kind of girl."

"And you like her that way."

"Yeah, but if she becomes another kind of girl at some point, I'll like her that way, too."

"Good thing," Zara says. "Because Ivy can be full of surprises."

"That she can."

She comes out of the bathroom with my pajamas slung low on her hips. Josephine is sanitizing the table we ate on. She had Dice and Cujo carry it inside. I bring a towel for Ivy to lie on.

"Will this thing hold me?" she asks.

"You'll be fine."

"Okay," she says. "I'm trusting you. You better be right."

She sits on the towel and wiggles a bit to test the strength of the table before she lies back. Josephine transfers her sketch to Ivy's skin and asks her if she wants to take a look at it in the mirror. "Nope. Tonight's about trust. If it looks right to you, then go for it."

Her eyes find mine for reassurance, and I smile. Being the one she looks to feels good. "I want to kiss it already."

Josephine shoots a warning look over her shoulder. "You are not allowed to put your mouth on this tattoo until it's fully healed."

Ivy tenses at the initial buzz of the tattoo gun. "You ready?" Josephine asks.

"I'm ready."

When the needles meet her skin, she squeezes her eyes shut, but she's still. I take her hand, and she opens her eyes. "Breathe. It helps."

"I know. I just forget sometimes."

I watch the ink spread in her skin. The flower almost looks like there's a flame behind it when Josephine layers shades of orange around the edges and blends the colors. It reminds me of the way the sun makes Ivy's hair glow, the way it changes in the light. She's going to love it.

Zara's tattoo is floral, too, but it's a shoulder cap so it takes a few hours. It's getting late, but I'm not ready for anyone to go. It's been a long time since I've hung out with more than one person at a time for longer than a community dinner or a meeting. I forgot how much I used to enjoy being in the company of friends.

Josephine doesn't ask Cujo what he wants when he sits for his tattoo. Either they've already discussed it or he trusts her a hell of a lot.

I sneak glances at his forearm while she works. It's a rattlesnake. Huh, I would've figured he already had one of those tattooed on him somewhere.

Ivy leans over to see what he's getting. "Ha! I should get one of those, too."

I laugh. "You and Cujo with matching rattlesnake tattoos would send April over the edge."

Josephine smirks. "Don't tempt me with a good time."

Dice says he'll take Zara home, and no one asks if he means to his casita or hers, but Ivy sure looks like she wants to know. "Call me when you're up tomorrow. We'll spend the whole day at the festival together."

When Josephine is all packed up, she and Cujo head out on his bike, leaving Ivy and me alone. "If you stay, I promise not to bother you for sex. I know that tattoo burns. Do you want something for the pain?"

"Maybe you could do something to try to take my mind off of it, and I could owe you one."

"One?"

She laughs. "I know. I probably already owe you dozens."

"You don't owe me anything, Ivy. You will never owe me anything. You're already in pajamas. You may as well stay."

"I'll stay. I might take these pajamas with me tomorrow. They're pretty comfy."

"They look better on you, anyway."

Ivy

No Illusions

JENSEN MAKES US CHEESY scrambled eggs for breakfast. It looks too early outside to be eating breakfast, but he says he has to be at the gate before people start showing up.

"Is this the only way you know how to cook eggs?"

"No. I can make them without cheese, too."

"Oh, good. If the winery doesn't work out, you can always open a restaurant."

"I bet a restaurant that served nothing but scrambled eggs would be a hit."

"Maybe a food truck. You could offer all sorts of toppings. Serve it on a folded waffle like a taco."

"Your brain really does just take an idea and run with it. It's impressive."

"Not everyone is impressed by it."

"They should be."

We finish our breakfast, and he drives me home to Sparrow's Song.

It's not quite sunrise, and I could use a few more hours of sleep, but if I crawl into my bed, I'll sleep half the day away. I take a shower instead, make some coffee, and sit on my back patio to watch the sun finish coming up.

A roadrunner zips toward me to snap up a scorpion that I hadn't seen. It was several feet away, so no threat, but I didn't know it was there until the roadrunner got it. Those birds are fearless. If they want it, they take it. Even rattlesnakes and horned toads. "Where were you when I was trying to get my laundry done?"

The roadrunner cocks its head at me with the scorpion still in its bill. Then it zooms off to a rock to finish disabling its prey. Nature is brutal.

I hear footsteps at the side of my casita. "Hello," I call out, hoping I'm talking to a human.

Zara laughs. "Aw, I didn't know you were outside. I was trying to sneak up to your back door and scare you."

"Did you have a good night with Dice?"

"You're not mad, are you?"

"No. Of course not."

She sits next to me. "He's fun."

"If you say so."

"What is that bird doing?"

"Beating a scorpion to death."

"Cool. Glad I asked. How is your tattoo?"

"Uncomfortable."

"It'll heal soon. And then you'll have a beautiful reminder of this place."

"I'm going to have a lot of those." The wind kicks up and causes my screen door to slap against the frame.

"You are still coming back home, right?"

"I am." I sip my coffee. "But I might quit my job."

"Noooo. To do what?"

"I don't know yet. Maybe I'll make soap. Or candles."

"You came all the way to the desert to become a beach hippie?"

"There are desert hippies, too."

"Please tell me you're not quitting as soon as you get home."

"No. I'm going to start using up my vacation days, though. I should've done that to come here instead of trying to work. Might've cleared my head sooner."

"I figured you'd be taking some vacation time to see Stinger's winery location and help him get that underway."

"I'll help if he asks. But it's his venture, not mine."

"I'm not sure he thinks of it that way. Besides, I could totally see you working in a winery."

"He has to build it first. Who knows where we'll be by then."

"You could ask your psychic neighbors."

"No, thank you. Do you want to ask them something?"

"Oh, I already have an appointment tomorrow evening at five."

"Of course you do. Do you think you'll see Dice after you leave here?"

"I doubt it. He's thinking about moving to Miami."

"You like the beach."

"And I like men who are temporary."

"That's how I used to like them, too."

"Yeah, but only because you'd had your heart broken. I've always preferred them that way."

A car engine sputters out front. "I wonder if that's someone showing up for the festival?"

"I think it's probably Dice heading out."

"Did you leave him asleep in your bed to come over here?"

"He's a grown man. He can find his way home. What was I supposed to do, wake him up and cook him breakfast? Please."

I laugh at how matter-of-factly she states her case. She sees the world exactly as it is. No illusions.

Sometimes, I think I've always been drawn to magical thinking, but other times, I think I've been too afraid to embrace it. According to Petra, my father was a lousy magician, but he pursued it anyway. The ordinary magic of the world wasn't enough for him, but he couldn't see that he wasn't really a showman. I think he was probably just a very tall but very small man in most regards. Maybe he still is.

Nothing is ever enough for people like that. They're always trying to prove themselves.

I don't feel like I have anything to prove, but I do want a little more magic in my life. The real kind. No illusions.

Cujo's bike starts up next door and rattles my teeth. I can tell by the direction the sound fades into that he's headed for the gate to help Jensen.

Josephine walks over. "I thought I heard y'all out here. Are you ready for the craziness of the festival?"

"If it gets too crazy, we can always hide out here," I offer.

"Yeah, but be sure to lock your doors," she says. "Even though there are signs stating which casitas are open studios, there's always at least one wanderer who will walk in on you in your own bathroom."

"Glad I showered already."

"Get ready. They'll invade soon."

We go inside and finish off the pot of coffee I made. "Where do we start?" I ask Josephine. "Should we walk over to Myrna's and keep her company until people show up?"

"No. Come on. We're walking up to the gate. You need to witness the arrival."

"Sounds ominous," Zara says.

Josephine smiles. "It's something."

I've never seen the gate closed, but it's shut this morning. Jensen and Cujo lean on it. They laugh and talk as if they don't know what's behind them.

"What the hell is happening?" I push up onto the balls of my feet and search for the end of the line. There is a trail of cars down the dirt road that leads into Ivydell. The line stretches beyond the mesa. I think it might go all the way to the highway. "Is this for real?"

"It's real."

"Where did they all come from?"

"Everywhere."

"How do they know when to show up?"

"Word of mouth, I guess."

"There isn't enough stuff for all these people to buy something."

"They don't all come to buy," she says. "Some just come to be here."

"This is the last time they'll ever get to do this." It feels like I'm witnessing something historic. In a way, I guess I am.

"Do you think we should tell them?"

"No. I know better now. They should be able to enjoy it until the bitter end."

Cujo pushes the gate open, and Jensen waves the first car forward. He says something to the driver that makes the guy smile and honk his horn as he drives in. When the next car hears his message, they honk, too.

Josephine smiles. "No entry fee this year. We don't need a maintenance fund anymore."

New horns join in as more cars drive past us. "Who knew not having to pay an entry fee could make people so happy?"

Zara shakes her head. "I think these people were happy when they got here. No entry fee just adds another layer."

Layers of happiness. What a magical fucking concept. But it's not an illusion. All these happy people are very, very real.

For the next forty-eight hours, I'm going to see Ivydell like I've never seen it before. And then it will get quiet again. And then I'll have to leave. And I'll never see it again.

I could've been happy not knowing. But I can be happy this way, too.

"Jensen said The Circle gets used for demonstrations and performances, but he never explained beyond that."

"They say what happens in The Circle stays in The Circle." Josephine waggles her eyebrows at me.

She's making a joke, but I know of a performance where that was the truth. Unless she knows, too, and that's the joke. *No secrets in Ivydell.*

I don't care if she knows. I don't care if the whole world knows. Maybe one day he and I will recreate the scene in a vineyard.

Wizard joins our group, dropping a dead lizard at my feet like a peace offering. Except it turns out it's only playing dead, and we all yelp when it hops up, hulks out, and hisses at the giant cat.

The lizard runs. The cat chases. The cars keep coming.

"I'm ready. Let's do this crazy thing."

Thank you for taking this third visit to Ivydell!

Are you ready to finally go to the festival? Book 4: Bitch, Please! It's Ivydell, the final book in this series, will take you there!

Also from **INDIE SPARKS**

Steamy Rom-Com Duologies:

VENGEFUL VIXENS:
Your Boss Says Hi!

She's only looking for a rebound guy, but her ex's boss plays for keeps. He's a former NFL player who used to have thousands of women screaming his name every week. Now, he only wants one woman to scream his name, and she just might become his biggest fan yet.

Your Trainer Says Hi!

She only wants to see her ex's beloved personal trainer in the gym—until he convinces her his hot tub could do wonders for her aching muscles. He isn't wrong, but between the heat, the bubbles, and his off-the-clock skills, she might be in too deep before she knows it. He's definitely not her type. So, why can't she stop seeing him?

NAUGHTY AT THE NOUVEAU:

Maintenance & Management

She's the new property manager. He's the new maintenance supervisor. They rub each other the wrong way . . . until they start to rub each other so very right. There's a non-fraternization policy, so they really shouldn't. But there's only one bed!

Landscaping & Leasing

He ghosted her after an unfortunate incident that she had absolutely no control over—and now, she's accidentally hired his landscaping company. She may not be completely immune to his charms (that voice!), but she's not weak enough to fall for him twice. But what if she doesn't know the whole story about why he disappeared from her life?

More Small Town Romance:

Peri

They were the wildest couple in town once, but that was a long time ago. They're not restless small-town kids anymore. And she's not back in town to see him. But seeing him once won't hurt anything. How much trouble could they get into as adults? Hardly any if you disregard the dirty karaoke and the lewd (allegedly) graffiti . . . and that old flame reigniting like an inferno.

www.ingramcontent.com/pod-product-compliance
Lightning Source LLC
Chambersburg PA
CBHW031337010826
48972CB00012B/832